MURDER IN CLIFDEN

DEREK FEE

For my Family

Copyright © 2021 by Derek Fee

All rights reserved.

No part of this book may be reproduced in any form or by any electronic or mechanical means, including information storage and retrieval systems, without written permission from the author, except for the use of brief quotations in a book review.

Publisher's Note: This is a work of fiction. Names, characters, places, and incidents are a product of the author's imagination. Locales and public names are sometimes used for atmospheric purposes. Any resemblance to actual people, living or dead, or to businesses, companies, events, institutions, or locales is completely coincidental.

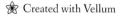 Created with Vellum

CHAPTER ONE

Detective Sergeant Fiona Madden lifted the cardboard cup out of the holder and looked at the gelatinous mess that half an hour before was labelled soup. She had no idea what it might taste like now and no desire to find out. It looked like frogspawn. She burped when she realised that half of it was nestling in her stomach, opened the car window and tossed the cup out.

'Ah, Sarge, the environment.'

She laughed. They were parked on a street in a council estate in the least desirable area of Galway where the discarded cup of soup would mingle with dirty nappies and used female sanitary products. She looked across at her partner, Detective Garda Sean Tracy. He was the embodiment of the PC generation and that meant political correctness and not police constable. But he was also a handsome devil with a head of dark curls, blue eyes, and a strong jaw. There was many a female in Galway who would jump at the chance to take her place beside Tracy in a darkened car at three o'clock in the morning. The scene in front of them was eerie, principally because someone had taken the time and energy to break most of the streetlights.

'Do you think we might be wasting our time?' Tracy looked through a pair of night-vision binoculars and focused on a white panel truck parked a hundred yards away on the dark street.

'If I thought that, I wouldn't be sitting here.' The panel truck that was the centre of their attention had been stolen in central Galway that morning and had been seen entering the council estate. Earlier in the day, Fiona and Tracy had located it parked in plain sight in front of a house. They could easily have recovered the van and arrested the occupants and the case of the stolen panel truck would have been solved. But there was a larger picture. Fiona had noted that in the case of two unsolved burglaries, a panel truck that had been used in the heists had been stolen on the morning of the raid. She had therefore proposed that they do not seize the truck but that they should put it under surveillance and catch the burglars in the act. Her boss, Detective Inspector Horgan, had reluctantly agreed which led to her and Tracy sitting together in an unmarked police car in the middle of the night. Since the plan had been hers, she was anxious and hoped that the gang would make their move soon.

Tracy dropped his binoculars into his lap and lay back in his seat. 'Not a peep.'

'It's the witching hour. They'll be on their way soon.' At least she hoped they would.

Almost as an answer to her prayer, there was the sound of a door opening and men's excited voices.

Tracy shot forward and took up his binoculars. 'Three men dressed in blue boiler suits with beanies on their heads.' He dropped the binoculars and reached his right hand for the ignition key.

'Easy now. Let them get organised and on their way. Then we'll slip in behind them.' She could see one of the men loading a gas canister into the rear of the van. Suddenly the headlights on the van lit up the street and them. There was no time to scrunch down so Fiona launched herself at Tracy and kissed him. The van moved off in their direction and the driver sounded the horn as they passed.

'Sorry about that,' Fiona said. 'Get the car started and get after them.'

Tracy was still trying to compose himself. 'That was a bit unexpected and not unpleasant.' He made a quick three-point turn and took off after the van.

Galway is a relatively small city and at three o'clock in the morning, traffic is light. Tracy managed to get himself into position fifty yards behind the van. They drove out of the estate and took Bothar na dTreabh towards the centre of the city. At the intersection for the Tuam Road, they turned right.

'Looks like you called this one correctly. Any idea where they're off to?'

'No.'

Halfway down the Tuam Road, Tracy got his answer when the van turned into the Liosbán Industrial Estate. He waited until the van had disappeared before following them into the warren of roads that made up the estate. He turned his lights off and cruised past the turns until Fiona tapped him on the arm.

'Turn around. They're at the end of the last street on the left.'

Tracy turned and stopped before the junction of the next road on the right. He and Fiona exited the car. Fiona threw Tracy a stab vest and put one on herself.

The van was parked near the end of the road with its lights off. There were two possible target industrial units, one on either side of the road. The three men exited the van, their beanies turned into balaclavas. There were two heavyset men and the third was smaller in stature. One of the heavyset men opened the rear of the van, unloaded the gas canister, and brought it to the front of the unit on the right. He set it directly against a metal grille. The smaller man took the driving seat and pulled the van down the road.

The man who had carried the canister bent and fiddled with the top. A naked flame appeared in his hand.

'They're going to blow the entrance.' Fiona sprinted towards the flaming canister closely followed by Tracy.

There were two men running away from them. 'Garda Síochána,' Tracy screamed.

Fiona was closing on the men when there was a large explosion and she was flung backwards by the compression wave. The gas canister was flung up in the air and the metal grille lay broken in the middle of the road. The quiet was replaced by the shrieking of an alarm.

The two heavyset men stopped dead and seemed to notice the police officer for the first time.

'Ram the fuckers,' one of them shouted at the van driver.

The van driver hit the accelerator and pointed the van at the two police officers.

'Watch out,' Fiona cried and took off after the two men.

Tracy jumped back as the van mounted the footpath and crashed into the gate of one of the units. The driver tried desperately to reverse but the van's bumper was stuck fast in the unit's railing. Tracy pulled the van door open, took hold of the driver's boiler suit and yanked him to the footpath. He removed a pair of handcuffs and cuffed the man to the shattered railing. Then he took off after his boss who was now a hundred yards ahead of him.

Fiona was only twenty yards behind when the two men reached the end of the road. They suddenly realised that it was a dead end. They turned and saw a small woman closing on them. Further down the road, the van was crashed into a unit and they could see a man sprinting in their direction. One of the men took a flick knife from the pocket of his boiler suit.

Fiona heard the metallic click of the knife opening and stopped. She stared at the two stationary figures. 'You're under arrest for breaking and entering at the moment. If you put away the knife, that's the way it'll stay.'

'Fuck you,' the man holding the knife said. He started towards her and lunged.

She easily avoided him. 'Bad decision.'

She kicked him in the hip as he went by. He was in midair when he aimed a slash at her face. She caught the hand holding the knife and twisted hard. The knife flew into the road clanging as it hit the concrete. She continued to twist until she heard the crack and knew that her assailant's wrist was broken. The second man stood like he was stuck to the ground while his colleague screamed in pain.

'Easy.' Tracy appeared at her side and held his arms wide. 'It's all over. Your mate in the van is handcuffed.'

Fiona handed Tracy her handcuffs and he cuffed the man facing them.

'The uniforms and an ambulance,' Fiona said. 'That poor man on the ground broke his wrist in the fall. As soon as they're loaded up, I'm away home to catch up on my sleep. You can get busy on the paperwork.'

CHAPTER TWO

Fiona felt herself being shaken awake. She rubbed the sleep from her eyes. 'It can't be midday already.'

'It can and it is,' Fiona's partner, Aisling McGoldrick was standing at the foot of the bed.

Fiona swivelled her legs and put them on the floor. 'I'm still half asleep. I hate this bloody job.'

'That's not true. You'd do it for nothing.'

Fiona stood. 'That's a bit of an exaggeration.'

'Your boss phoned twenty minutes ago. He'd like to see you when you get to the station.

'There's no peace for the wicked. I need a shower.'

'I'll make you a cup of coffee and a ham sandwich while you're getting dressed.' She headed in the direction of the kitchen. 'God knows when you'll get your next meal.'

After the shower, Fiona felt human and tucked into the sandwich and coffee.

'So, you got the bad guys?'

'Yeah, but not before they blew the shit out of the front of Higgins Electrical. The owner would have preferred if we had prevented the explosion. There's CCTV so we won't have a problem getting them put away. One of them pulled a knife on me.'

'I bet he paid for that.'

'I think I might have broken his wrist. What did Horgan say?'

'Nothing much, the message was short and sweet.'

'That's the boss.' She finished her meal. 'He's a bit of a slavedriver.'

'What's the plan for this evening?'

'Rest and recuperation. Try and think of something where we do no work and have lots of fun.' She kissed Aisling. 'Thanks for the sandwich and coffee. I'd better hit the road.'

FIFTEEN MINUTES LATER, Fiona drove her Kawasaki 650 into the parking lot of Mill Street station and parked her ride in its usual spot. Up to a few months before she had been the proud owner of a vintage Vincent Black Shadow but that was a thing of the past. Her current ride wasn't a replacement but it fitted her budget.

The duty sergeant gave her a thumbs up as she entered. 'I heard about the collar at the Liosban Estate. You're some lady.'

Fiona put on a shocked face 'Nobody thinks of me as a lady.'

'It appears that one of the robbers had a bad fall and broke his wrist.'

'What a pity.' She started up the stairs.

Most TV crime dramas depict police work as being composed of car chases, drug busts, shootouts, sexual encounters and giving evidence in court. Policework is drudgery and paperwork. It requires unlimited patience to trawl through reams of financial data or hours watching CCTV to find a clue leading to an arrest. That reality was visible in the CID room at Mill Street station. The members of the Criminal Investigation

Division were hard at work in front of their computer terminals or examining six-inch folders packed with documents. She'd opt for *Starsky and Hutch* any day of the week. Tracy was half asleep at his desk. She looked over his shoulder and saw that he had almost finished a report on their nocturnal activities. She switched on her computer. She had received the footage from the CCTV cameras at Higgins Electrical. She'd get a print of some of the more spectacular frames and add them to the file. The duty sergeant at Salthill had sent her a copy of the charge sheet for the two men in custody and the third man would be transferred from the hospital to the cells during the afternoon.

'Didn't you get my message?'

She recognised Horgan's dulcet tones. 'For God's sake, boss, stop creeping up on people.'

'I hear your partner is a professor at the university. With all her degrees, couldn't she even give you a simple message?'

'Congratulations, sergeant,' Fiona said. 'On your successful operation this morning.'

'Okay, congratulations, sergeant, on your successful operation this morning. Now, why didn't you come to see me like I asked.'

'I've just arrived and I was on my way upstairs when you waylaid me. By the way, we received the CCTV from Higgins Electrical. Those three lads are in the bag.'

'Good, because I've got an important job for you.'

Fiona got one of her funny feelings. When the boss proffers an important job there's generally a catch.

'Our colleagues in Clifden are finding themselves in the middle of a mini crime wave. There has been a series of break-ins at holiday homes in the area and there's been an outbreak of antisocial behaviour, rocks being thrown at passing cars, fighting in the streets. You know the kind of thing. The peace-loving citizens would be reassured if there was a visit from a couple of Garda detectives.'

'Boss, Tracy and I are expected in Salthill to interview the three boys we nabbed. It's our collar and we should follow up.'

'The follow-up has already been reassigned. The job in Clifden is important.'

'I don't like where this is going,' Fiona said. 'There wouldn't be members of a certain community in the area, would there?'

'The Clifden Horse Fair takes place tomorrow and there are two tinker families camped in the area. I want you and Tracy to go to Clifden and talk to them.'

'To what end?' Fiona asked. 'It won't stop the break-ins. It's a bloody public relations exercise. We should be spending our time on following up the Higgins' raiders.'

'I'll be the judge of how you should be spending your time and I want you to get your arse in gear and get to Clifden and do your job. Do I make myself clear?'

'As a bell.' Fiona picked up her jacket and motioned to Tracy who had been following the conversation.

'So much for lunch,' Tracy mumbled.

CHAPTER THREE

Clifden is a coastal town in County Galway, in the region of Connemara, located on the Owenglin River where it flows into Clifden Bay. As the largest town in the region, it is often referred to as "the capital of Connemara". If that title were true, it would be the least inhabited capital in the world. There are only one thousand five hundred inhabitants. The Gaelic speaking majority of the area would contest that denomination since Clifden is bang in the centre of an English-speaking enclave.

Fiona and Tracy picked up a car in Mill Street and headed west.

'I sometimes think Horgan hates me,' Fiona said.

'I get the impression that he really likes you. You're pissed off because he interfered with your lunch plans.'

'I'm pissed off because we're being used as window dressing. We have real work back in Galway interviewing the burglars. That's police work. Horgan is trying to cheat us out of our collar.'

'You know that's not why you're so antsy. You always react negatively when we need to go into Connemara. I wonder why that is?'

'Maybe there's a reason I react negatively. I have a lot of unpleasant memories. When I visit various sites, old ghosts that I thought were buried reappear.'

'I can relate to the unpleasant memories but surely you don't believe in the ghosts bullshit.'

She'd told nobody that she could see them as clearly as if they were standing in front of her. 'There are more things in heaven and earth, young Tracy, than are dreamt of in your philosophy.'

'You're a strange fish, Fiona.'

'You're a strange fish, *sergeant*.'

'Okay, sergeant, how come you can pull out a quote like that from Hamlet?'

'We studied it for the Inter Cert. It was my last year in school. I've never forgotten that play.' She hadn't forgotten the whole year. It was the year where everything changed. There would be no more plans to go to university and become a doctor. She'd always known that there would never be a husband and two point four children. But other plans disappeared like a will o' the wisp over a bog on a foggy night. 'I often wonder if Shakespeare were alive today, what genre would he write.'

'Historical or murder mystery.'

'Enough bonding.' Fiona leaned back and closed her eyes.

'WHERE TO EXACTLY?' Tracy said as they entered Clifden.

'Let's start at the police station. Perhaps they know something about this crime wave.'

Clifden police station is located on the Galway side of the town in a modern one-storey building. Tracy pulled into a parking space.

They entered a small reception area.

'Sergeant Glennan about?' Fiona asked the young Garda on reception.

'Who wants to know?'

She produced her warrant card. 'Detective Sergeant Madden wants to know.'

The young Garda blushed. 'Sorry, sergeant.' He pushed a button and the door to their left buzzed.

Tracy pushed it and held it open for her.

'He's in his office at the rear of the station.'

Fiona led the way and stopped before an office with a brass plate bearing Glennan's name. The door opened before she could knock.

'You're welcome.' Glennan was smiling broadly as he opened the door to permit them to enter. 'Come in and sit down. Horgan told me you were on the way.'

Fiona sat on a chair facing Glennan's desk. 'It's not like you to ask for help from Galway.'

'We have a unique situation. Aside from the usual tourists, we have two groups of travellers camped outside the town. Apparently, they don't get on which is a diplomatic way of saying that there is a long-running feud between them. Over the past few days, we've had five burglaries, arrested twenty people for drunk and disorderly, had a spate of stones being thrown through windows and at cars and more than forty complaints describing antisocial behaviour. This town exists on the summer trade and the local Chamber of Commerce have complained to the minister who has complained to the commissioner who has threatened to cut me a new arsehole if I don't deal with the situation. I reckoned Horgan owed me over the Glenmore murder and that's why you're here. Now, would either of you like a cup of tea?'

'I think we should get on with it,' Fiona said. 'What do you want us to do?'

'Wield the big stick. You're not plain coppers. You're CID.'

'What have you got so far?'

Glennan picked up a bunch of buff-coloured files and

handed them to her. 'Five burglaries; the doors have been forced with either a jemmy or a sizeable screwdriver. None of the residences were alarmed. They were summer homes so there wasn't too much in the way of valuables about. They got away with electrical items, TVs, stereos, that kind of stuff. Things that can be sold on to some idiot in a pub.'

Fiona flipped through the photos in the files. The houses were small and sparsely furnished, typical of the holiday homes in the area. The electrical items wouldn't be top grade but the burglaries were a safe bet. Nobody in residence and no neighbours to call the local constabulary. She handed the files to Tracy. 'Any fingerprints?'

'Lots,' Glennan said. 'So many that elimination would be a nightmare. The owners were letting the properties and weren't so fastidious with the cleaning. They'll present an inflated insurance claim and forget about the burglary.'

'They won't feel personally violated?'

'No, only when the insurance asks them to produce receipts.'

'Could be the work of kids.'

'Could be, but the goods would be passed to someone older.'

'And there's no local Fagin?'

'If there was, I'd know him.'

'The searchlight falls on the travellers.'

'That's what the local members of the Chamber of Commerce think. They don't give a curse about the value of the stolen goods. It's the good name of the town that counts.'

'I don't like the idea of being the heavy hand of the law where culpability is not clear.'

'You don't have to be heavy. Just let them know that Big Brother is watching.'

'Where are the groups camped?'

'One of them has their caravans parked on the Sky Road. Some smart alec has parked them on our most touristic route.

The second group have a site on the Errislannan Peninsula near Drinagh.'

'Are there no approved sites in the area?'

'No.'

'Are you coming with us?'

'No, I've already tried my hand at it. I'll send one of the lads along.'

'Not the green copper on reception.'

Glennan smiled as he nodded.

THE SKY ROAD in Clifden takes a circular route leading from Clifden into the Kingstown Peninsula and along the Atlantic Ocean. Outside the town at Castle Demesne, it separates into the lower and upper roads. The lower road runs downhill towards the sea and it was on this road that the Connors clan had set up their camp.

Tracy pulled in across the road from the fifteen modern mobile homes and assorted high-end SUVs bearing UK registrations parked on the Sky Road. There was a substantial amount of trash already distributed around the scenic area. Fiona, Tracy and the fresh-faced Garda from reception named Costello strolled across the road into the encampment. The looks they received from the travellers seated on camp chairs wasn't friendly. A boy who couldn't be more than six years old walked up to them and shouted, 'Fuck off coppers.' He turned around, dropped his pants, exposed his behind, and wiggled it.

Fiona fake smiled. 'They start early.'

Tracy laughed and Costello looked glum.

'Run off and get your daddy,' Fiona said.

'Mam, fucking coppers!' the child shouted at the top of his voice.

A woman exited from one of the caravans. She was beautiful and had long curly brown hair. Her ensemble would give nightmares to a stylist. Her feet were immersed in two oversized black wellington boots, above the boots was a multicoloured gypsy skirt and above that was a faded black Trinity College hoodie. She marched over to the three police officers. 'Why are you picking on my child? He's only a baby.'

'We're not picking on him,' Fiona said. 'He introduced us to his bare backside as soon as we approached. I don't think he has a high opinion of police officers.'

'Maybe he's had a few bad experiences with them.'

'Or maybe he's listening to his parents.'

'He's been moved on forcibly enough times to have formed his own opinion of the police.'

'We're not here to move anyone on.' Fiona took out her warrant card. 'Detective Sergeant Fiona Madden and this young man is Detective Garda Sean Tracy. The man in uniform is Garda Costello from Clifden station. And you are?'

'Maggie Connors. If you're not here to move us on, why are you here?'

'It appears that there's a mini crime wave in Clifden and we've been sent to look into it.'

'And this is the first place you come when you're looking into it?'

'Yes, and it won't be the last,' Fiona said. 'The good citizens of Clifden are up in arms. Their quiet lives have been disrupted and they fear the tourist trade will be damaged.'

'So, the finger-pointing starts with the travellers. The local residents won't sleep safe in their beds until we leave. Is that the story?'

'No, the story is that the law is being broken.'

Connors pointed at Costello. 'Isn't he local law enforcement? Why are CID involved?' 'Beyond my pay grade.' There was a noise behind Fiona and she turned as a white panel van and a new Range Rover with an English registration pulled into the camp.

The driver of the Range Rover exited and strode in their direction. He ignored the police officers and spoke directly to

Maggie. 'What's going on here? What are the police doing here?'

'Don't get your cacks in a knot, Phil,' Maggie said. 'The officers are making inquiries about a crime wave in Clifden. There's no need to come across all macho. They're only doing their job.'

Fiona took out her warrant card and did the introductions. 'And who would you be?' The new arrival was about the same age as the woman. He had a full head of dark hair and wore a pair of rough-wool trousers and a donkey jacket. He was handsome in a rugged way except for the scar that ran along his left cheek. Fiona had been in the game long enough to recognise that it was a result of his cheek meeting with a knife. He was over six foot and built to match.

He ignored the Garda presence and pulled his wife aside. They held a whispered conversation that lasted several minutes.

'Please excuse my husband Phil,' Maggie Connors said. 'He likes the police even less than my son.' She turned to her husband. 'I was just about to invite the officers for a cup of tea so they could tell us about this crime wave and how we could help them. I'm sure you have something important to do.'

'Get them out of here.'

Maggie touched him on the shoulder and he walked off in the direction of the white van muttering to himself.

Fiona noted that Phil Connors deferred to his wife and she wondered whether this was a traveller tradition. It was strange to see such a large and fearsome man being treated like a child by a woman.

Maggie moved in the direction of her caravan. 'Let's have a cup of tea and you can ask me whatever questions you like.'

'That's exceedingly kind of you.'

Maggie was standing at the door of a new-looking caravan. Fiona walked forward closely followed by Tracy and Costello.

The inside of the large caravan was spotless. They entered

a space at one end that consisted of a small but well-stocked kitchen and a dining alcove.

'Take a seat.' Maggie indicated the bench seating and turned the gas on beneath the kettle. Tracy and Costello slid into the centre and left the two ends of the L-shaped seat to the ladies.

'Nice caravan,' Fiona said.

'It's a bit cramped when the kids are here.' Maggie poured hot water into a teapot and placed it on the table. She took four mugs from a press and passed them around before opening a fridge and producing a bottle of milk. 'Luckily, two of the kids are with their grandparents in Dublin.'

'Detective Tracy, why don't you play mother,' Fiona said. 'Their grandparents are settled.'

Tracy shot Fiona a filthy look before pouring four mugs of tea.

Maggie laughed. She put a plate of biscuits on the table. 'They're my parents and they've always been settled. They've lived in the same house for the past forty years.'

'You're not a traveller?'

'The fleece says it all, Trinity College class of 2003. I studied sociology and my first job was with the National Travellers Service. I met Phil and I've been a traveller ever since.'

'Have you ever heard the song 'The Raggle Taggle Gypsy?'.' Fiona sipped her tea.

'I suppose I'm the living proof that the travellers have charms that get us women to follow them. It sounds romantic but the reality can prove to be more mundane. But then again Phil is no raggle-taggle gypsy. His family have been travellers for generations. So, Fiona, what can we do for you.'

Fiona noticed an amount of eye contact that was taking place between Maggie and Tracy. She glanced at Tracy and his eyes flicked away from Maggie. 'You could tell me what you know about the spate of burglaries and the outbreak of antisocial behaviour in a town of one thousand six hundred peaceful souls.'

'That would be a short conversation because I know nothing about either the burglaries or the antisocial behaviour. But I do think your visit is associated with the view among the settled community that travellers are responsible for crime. I think they call it ethnic profiling.'

'I can assure you that the Garda Síochána are immune to the concept of ethnic profiling. For the moment, our assumption is that it's a coincidence that the mini crime wave began when the travellers arrived.'

'That's exactly what it is, a coincidence.'

Fiona looked at Tracy. 'I don't believe in coincidences but there are exceptions.'

'We're here for the horse fair and nothing else.'

'I didn't see any horses in the camp. Are you here to buy?'

'It's more of a social gathering. We're here to meet old friends.'

'Apparently, you have some old enemies around also.'

'The Fureys.'

Fiona nodded. 'That could lead to trouble.'

'Nobody wants trouble. We'll be staying away from each other.'

Fiona finished her tea and stood. 'We'll leave you in peace.'

Tracy and Costello stood.

'I assume you'll be speaking with the Fureys.'

'We will.'

They exited the caravan together.

'We'll be looking at everyone we think might be involved in criminality.' Fiona walked towards the car but stopped when an old female traveller approached the group. Fiona guessed that she might be in her seventies or maybe eighties. Her grey hair was unkempt and formed a fan around her face on which there wasn't a wrinkle.

She stood in front of Fiona. 'I saw you arrive.'

'Come now, Peggy.' Maggie Connors tried to come between them but the old lady pushed her away.

Peggy pointed one of her bony fingers at Fiona. 'There's a black shadow over you. It follows you wherever you go. There's death around you. I can smell it on you.' She spat on the ground at Fiona's feet.

'Enough now.' Maggie said. 'They're police officers.'

'I know that.' The old lady turned back to Fiona. 'Truth will out.'

Maggie turned to Fiona. 'Pay her no mind.'

A CHILL RAN down Fiona's spine and she needed to get away from the old lady's eyes that bored into her. She strode towards the car closely followed by Tracy and Costello. At the car, she turned and looked back. The old lady was still staring at her.

Tracy drove the car out of the camp. 'Where to?'

Fiona looked at Costello. 'Where's the other group camped?'

'On the other side of town close to the Old School House.'

'Do I have to go through the centre of town?' Tracy asked.

'Yes.'

'Then I think a pit stop is in order,' Fiona said.

MAGGIE CONNORS and the old woman stood watching as the car left the encampment. 'You put the heart across that poor woman,' Maggie said. 'What was that bullshit about the shadow and death?'

'You of all people know better than to doubt Peggy. There's a deep dark secret hanging over that woman and it involves death.'

'You've been playing with the tarot cards again. Save it for the punters at the horse fair tomorrow.'

'I didn't need the cards. I could see it on her.'

CHAPTER FOUR

Fiona sat on the toilet in EJ King's pub in Clifden. She excused herself as soon as she, Tracy and Costello entered. She didn't need the toilet. She needed to be alone. The old traveller woman had got to her. She shivered when she remembered the look in the old woman's eyes. There was something about the Irish and the belief in the powers of second sight. It was generally something stupid that triggered a deep emotion, a chance remark that struck a visceral memory that lies hidden well below the surface. A memory you want to keep buried. Maggie Connors was probably right. Peggy was a crazy old lady. But what she had said hit Fiona in a place that she was vulnerable. Was it possible that the old traveller had the ability to scrutinise her soul and had seen a blackness there? If she had, would she know that Fiona had spent eighteen years trying to forget she had given birth to a son who was the product of a rape? The arrival of a young man claiming to be the son she had given away for adoption had brought to the surface memories that she had suppressed. The old woman had hit a nerve. Did she know that the man who raped Fiona had disappeared soon after the birth of her son and was never seen or heard from again?

Fiona's memory of that period of her life was hazy. She had often dreamt of taking revenge on her rapist. Sometimes the dreams were so real that she wondered whether they had been dreams or repressed memories. There were things in her past that frightened her. She had sloughed off the parts that she didn't want to remember. Except that Fiona was unclear about the disappearance of her rapist and the truth behind it. Her mother kept banging on about postpartum psychosis. But Fiona now knew that she had been suffering from rape trauma syndrome. And part of that syndrome leads to a disruption of normal physical, emotional, cognitive and interpersonal relations. She could have done anything while in that state. The old woman had associated her with death and indicated that truth would out. She didn't want to know the truth. She feared the truth. She had a life. She was making a career in the Garda Síochána and she had fallen in love with another woman. She didn't want to think that there might be repercussions from her irrational past behaviour. That was the dichotomy. Her job was to bring murderers to justice but she was vague about whether she herself might have assisted in a murder. She stood up and flushed the toilet.

Fiona slid into the booth and pushed Tracy to make more room. 'What did you think of Maggie Connors?'

'A formidable lady,' Tracy said. 'What the hell is she doing with that Neanderthal? Did you see the scar on his cheek? It looked like he came out second best in a knife fight.'

'I wouldn't be so sure he came out second best. I suppose you noticed the character in the van.'

'Didn't take much notice of him.' Tracy bit into a ciabatta sandwich. He pushed his plate towards Fiona. 'I wasn't sure what you wanted. You can have half of mine.'

She patted him on the head. 'The perfect gentleman but an unobservant copper.'

'The guy never got out of the van.'

'Did you ever think that maybe there was a reason for that?'

Tracy stopped chewing and his face reddened.

'It's our job to notice everything and everybody. He was balding which is rare for a traveller. Ruddy complexion, stocky build, oval face and light beard. He was too far away to get the exact colour of his eyes but they looked dark.' She picked up half of the sandwich and took a bite. 'I think we might be seeing him again.'

'You think the Connors are involved in the burglaries?' Tracy said.

'I wouldn't be surprised. It might be a case of what Maggie doesn't know won't harm her.' She finished her tea. 'There are a lot of summer houses in this area and not all the owners had the foresight to install an alarm. It's a burglar's paradise. I don't think that our appearance is going to change anything. The locals will bleat about the break-ins and the antisocial behaviour but the travellers will move on when the horse fair is over and law and order will be re-established.'

'Nobody will go to jail?' Tracy said.

Fiona smiled. 'So young and so naïve. We're talking about buttons. Nobody cares about a ten-year-old TV. Let's get on to the second site. I want to finish and get back to town. Horgan has stiffed us on this one.'

'I need to use the toilet before we leave,' Costello said.

'It speaks,' Fiona said.

Costello stood. 'The sergeant told me to keep my mouth shut and my ears open. I'm just obeying instructions.'

'You're excused,' Fiona said. 'You can go to the toilet.'

THE SECOND ENCAMPMENT was located on the Errislannan Peninsula on a scenic stretch of road that faced Clifden Bay. The irony was that while the two traveller camps were separated by the waters of Clifden Bay, on a clear day one camp could look directly into the other. Fiona counted fifteen modern caravans parked in a line. Interspersed with the caravans were several top-of-the-range cars all bearing UK registrations. The Furey camp was a carbon copy of the neighbours across the bay.

Tracy parked the car at the end of the line of caravans. Fiona noticed a certain reluctance on Costello's part to exit with her and Tracy. The space behind the caravans had been turned into a living area with camp chairs and tables distributed around. There was the usual large number of children roughhousing and playing a ball game. Fiona walked forward to a table where four men were playing cards. Even though three people, one of whom was wearing a police uniform, were approaching, none of the men bothered to look in their direction. Two of the men were young, scarcely out of their late teens. They wore singlets which showed off heavily tattooed, muscular arms and hairy chests. Both were dark-haired and had swarthy complexions. They didn't look like they smiled often. The two other men were older, one possibly in his fifties and the second thirty years younger. They had the same hair colour and complexions as the younger men. The man in his twenties had a badly broken nose and a face that had taken a recent beating.

'Good afternoon, gentlemen.' Fiona produced her warrant card. 'Detective Sergeant Fiona Madden and these two stalwart lads are Detectives Garda Tracy and Garda Costello.'

The men continued their game and jabbered away in a language that Fiona had never heard before. It bore some relation to Gaelic but that was a language she spoke fluently. She wondered if they spoke English. 'Who is in charge here?'

The men ignored her.

She walked over to the table and put her warrant card in the middle on top of the money that had been placed as a stake. She stared at the older man. 'Don't be an arsehole. The sooner we finish our business here the sooner you'll be back to your game.'

The older man said something incomprehensible to the younger men and they vacated their seats. 'I'm Ted Furey.' He touched the man beside him on the sleeve of his jacket. 'This is my son Boxer. Put your arse in a chair and state your business.'

Fiona sat and motioned for Tracy to join her. The two Fureys resembled each other. Both were well-built and stocky. The elder man's grey hair stuck out from beneath a battered trilby hat that was perched rakishly on the top of his head. Boxer had the same curly hair but of a darker colour. Their faces were hard and unsmiling. 'We've come out from Galway to give our local colleagues a hand. It appears that there's a mini crime wave in Clifden.'

'What's that got to do with us?'

'The crime wave coincided with your arrival.'

'You mean there was no crime in Clifden before we arrived?'

'Burglaries up by five hundred per cent. Unruly behaviour in the streets up by a thousand per cent, drunk and disorderly arrests up eight hundred per cent. All coinciding with your arrival. That's a bit of a coincidence and I don't believe in coincidence. Nobody has been jailed up to now but that might change. That's what we're here to prevent.'

'We're not responsible for any of this crime wave. There's been a bit of drinking and horseplay down in the town but nothing you wouldn't have under normal circumstances. We're not the only travellers in the parish.'

'I've already spoken to the Connors. They got the same message.'

'They're a pack of mangey bastards. You'd do well to keep your eye on them.'

'I understand you and the Connors don't like each other. I've heard tell that there's a feud between you?'

'No, that's all behind us.'

'That's news to the Garda Síochána. Where did Boxer pick up his facial injuries?'

'A bare-knuckle fight in Galway. All above board.'

'Nobody wants any trouble. The horse fair is tomorrow and you'll be on your way the day after. Are we agreed?'

'We'll keep quiet but we can't guarantee the Connors won't start something.'

Fiona stood. 'I'm only here to give you the message that the chief superintendent is on the case and I'd prefer it if we didn't have to come back.'

'Message received,' Furey said. 'Can we get back to our game?' He nodded at the two young men.

'Thanks for the support,' Fiona said to Costello as they walked back to the car.

Castello opened his mouth to speak but Fiona cut him off. 'I know, keep your mouth shut and your ears open. God, the testosterone was beginning to catch in the back of my throat.'

'They look like a rough bunch,' Tracy said. 'I wouldn't like to meet Boxer in a dark alley.'

'Perish the thought. I think Mrs Connors beguiled you. But don't be fooled by her. The Connors clan are every bit as tough as the Fureys. I'd like to think that we might have accomplished something but I guess that Costello and his colleagues might have their work cut out for them before the horse fair is over.'

CHAPTER FIVE

As Fiona approached her cottage in the evening, she did an automatic check to see whether her son was sitting on the wall. It had only happened once in eighteen years but the event was so ingrained in her mind that she expected it to happen again at any moment. There was no sign of anyone in the vicinity of the cottage and she breathed a sigh of relief. She had only been a mother for a short period and that suited her fine. Her son had stolen her most prized possession, the vintage Vincent Black Shadow that had been lovingly restored by her grandfather. She could have reported the Black Shadow as stolen but she reckoned that the child she'd abandoned at birth had at least a right to what he took. She eased her motorbike through the gates and parked it in front of the cottage. It was a fine summer evening so she dumped her helmet on the saddle and walked down the lane in the direction of the sea. The air was full of ozone and she sucked great gulps into her lungs. There were only two houses between her cottage and the sea and both were in use as holiday homes. The family from Dublin that owned the first of the houses was in their garden and the man of the house was busy firing up his barbecue while his children were passing a hurling sliotar between them. It was a decent family scene and Fiona didn't envy them a bit. The second house was unoccupied and had been for several years now. Perhaps the family that owned it preferred Corfu or Malta to Connemara for their vacations. She could understand the desire to see strange places but she never tired of the place of her birth. She reached the shore, sat on a rock and stared at the Aran Islands out at sea. She had been thinking about the visit to the travellers' camps since she left Clifden. Like Glennan, she had no doubt that either or both sets of travellers were responsible for the break-ins and the antisocial behaviour but there wasn't a lot that could be done about it. As they returned Costello to the station, she had gone over a list of the items that had been stolen during the burglaries. There wasn't a single item of value. In fact, the whole haul might have amounted to a few hundred euros and could be fenced in a pub for considerably less. She and Tracy had been window dressing or an exercise in public relations. It only demonstrated that police work wasn't about the big cases but also the insignificant day-to-day work that would stultify many people. She remembered an item on a radio programme several weeks prior. In a small town in the US, a candidate for the job as a policeman had scored high on the entrance test. It was decided not to hire him because it was felt that he would become bored with the banality of police work. In other words, he was too smart to be a cop. At the time she'd wondered how that would reflect on her. She loved what she did but there was no doubt that there were elements of the job that would try the patience of a saint. The current joke concerning Mill Street station was that the mill grinds but it grinds slowly. The travellers and their impact on the small town of Clifden were at the back of her thoughts as she gazed across the ocean. The words of the old woman reverberated around her mind.

'A penny for them.'

Fiona started when she heard the voice behind her and smiled when she recognised her partner's accent.

Aisling McCluskey leaned down and kissed her. 'You were away with the fairies there.'

'You'd be selling yourself short if you paid a penny for what passes for thoughts in my head.'

Aisling sat down. 'It's beautiful this time of day. The sun sinking in the west and the islands out to sea lit by the orange-red glow.'

'This is my perfect place.'

'You're preoccupied lately.

'Maybe I'm waiting for the hammer to fall. Tim's out there somewhere.' She didn't bother to add that she had exposed her greatest secret to him that she knew where his father and her rapist was buried.

'Then you'll just have to keep living until it does. Make a start by absorbing the beauty that's around us.'

They both looked out to sea.

'When are we going to have "the conversation",' Aisling said, still staring at the scenery.

'What conversation?'

'The one where you talk about the devil that drives you. Where did the lust for justice come from?'

'You're talking like a clinical psychologist and I'm not a client.'

'I'm talking as your friend and lover. There's a demon eating you up and you need to confront it.'

'Have you heard of rape trauma syndrome?'

'Of course I have.'

'Well I've lived it. The numbness, the paralysing anxiety, the flight from reality and the drug use. Maybe you're right and I need to identify why I am what I am. I don't want to go there with you or anyone else.'

'You need professional help.'

'So do we all. Including you. Speaking of help, do you have a colleague who has expertise in the area of the travelling community?'

'One of the sociology professors deals with minority communities. He should fit the bill. When do you want to see him?'

'Yesterday. I've had a tough day. Can we delay the conversation?'

Aisling nodded.

'Good, I need a hot bath and a cold glass of white wine. Care to join me?'

Aisling smiled. 'You're incorrigible, you know that.'

'It's been said.'

CHAPTER SIX

Fiona had slept fitfully. Her mind was still replaying the meeting with the old traveller lady. She didn't want to believe in psychic ability but for months after her rapist disappeared, she'd been sure that she had seen a figure resembling him staring at her house from across the road. At the time, she'd put it down to the dullness in her sensory and memory functions that followed her rape. The dead do not rise and walk the earth. By five o'clock, she'd given up on sleep. She drove into Galway, waited until the dojo opened and spent two hours giving lessons before making her way to Mill Street. When she entered the squad room, her hair was still wet and her skin tingling from the exertion and the shower. Tracy was already at his desk and looking into space. 'She's not too old for you.' Fiona put two takeaway coffees on the desk. 'She could be your older sister.'

'What the hell are you talking about?'

'Maggie Connors, I assume that's who you're daydreaming about.'

'Will you catch yourself on, she's old enough to be...'

'Your older sister.'

Tracy laughed and took one of the coffees. 'I wasn't thinking about her.'

Fiona flopped into her chair. 'Don't lie to me. I'm a detective and I can recognise a lie a mile off.'

'I assume you've been to the dojo.' Tracy blew on his coffee. 'I recognise the endorphin high. Also, the wet hair and the scrubbed skin.' He toasted her with his cardboard cup. 'Thanks for the coffee.'

'My pleasure, just don't get used to it.'

'What's the plan?'

'Let's see what the day brings.'

Tracy shook his head before tasting his brew. 'Don't tell me you're still pissed off at Horgan for taking the collar away from us.'

'You bet I am.' She opened her computer and brought up her emails. 'There were two more burglaries in Clifden and a bit of a rumble between the young Connors and Furey lads. So much for our public relations exercise. Nobody took a blind bit of notice of us.

'What will Horgan do?'

'Nothing, it's a storm in a teacup,' Fiona said. 'The value of the stolen articles wouldn't buy you a decent dinner. Serves the owners of the cottages right. They use the places a couple of weeks a year and outfit their second homes with shit. My guess is that the miscreants are kids. No self-respecting burglar would steal a ten-year-old television. You'd have to pay someone to take it off your hands.'

The squad room door opened and Horgan entered. He marched straight to Fiona's desk.

'I saw the email from Glennan,' he said. 'Two more burglaries and a riot. The tinkers have been at it again.'

Fiona turned to face her boss. 'I don't think we can call a bit of pushing and shoving a riot.'

'Sorry, boss,' Tracy joined the conversation. 'The word you

were looking for is travellers. It's not politically correct to call them tinkers or itinerants.'

'Or knackers,' Fiona said.

'They're as Irish as anyone in this room,' Tracy said. 'And as such, they shouldn't be stigmatised with pejorative names.'

Horgan and Fiona looked at each other.

'That's the benefit of a college education, boss.' Fiona said. 'That was two four-syllable words in the one sentence. Fact is a good-looking woman traveller gave us a cup of tea and Sean took a liking to her.'

Tracy blushed.

'So, no follow up,' Horgan said.

'We did the necessary,' Fiona said. 'That doesn't mean the break-ins will stop. Empty cottages are easy targets. The horse fair is today. There'll be a lot of drunk and disorderly this evening and tonight so I doubt that the travellers will be in a fit state to move on tomorrow. The crime wave may last a day or two more but I'm sure Glennan and his lads will be able to handle it.'

'Good,' Horgan said. 'The boy with the broken wrist is being interviewed this morning at Salthill and Regan called in sick. I want Tracy to go over and take the second chair. Now.'

Tracy took his jacket from the back of his chair.

FROM A WINDOW on the top floor of Mill Street, Fiona watched Tracy as he exited the building and strode off in the direction of Salthill.

'I never pictured you as the mother hen type,' Horgan said from behind her.

'You told me to take care of him.'

'The word from the Park is that he'll go far. He won't be here long until they move him to a more visible role. In the meantime, try and make sure that he doesn't screw up.'

'What's the word from the Park on me?'

'You really don't want to know.'

'That bad?'

'You're a good detective but you tend to cut corners. The boys and girls in the Park like officers who follow the rules and procedures. They don't like mavericks. There's nothing wrong with being a detective sergeant.'

'During our visit to Clifden, I noticed that most of the cars had English registrations. The two traveller families are based somewhere in England.'

'Keep me informed.' He left the office.

Fiona sat at her desk. Most women officers knew that there was a glass ceiling. There were a few high-profile women at the top of the organisation but in general, the men preferred to think of their female colleagues as useful secretaries and tea makers. Perhaps the boys in the Park were wrong. If Tracy was going to be a shooting star, she could do worse than hitch her wagon to him.

CHAPTER SEVEN

The National University of Ireland at Galway was founded in 1845 as Queen's College Galway. It is located close to the centre of the city so Fiona decided to walk. It hadn't been a productive day and she sometimes found that a stroll through the city blew some of the cobwebs away. It would take a pretty strong breeze to deal with the fuzz that clogged her brain today. She had half an hour for a fifteen-minute walk so she crossed the river at Bridge Street and sauntered along Shop Street. Galway in summer was something else. A madhouse of people cramming the narrow, cobbled streets, Shop Street being the epicentre. The street performers make the situation worse. At the top of the street, ten young men are belting out a continuous stream of jigs and reels for an entranced crowd. Ten yards away, a woman is juggling wooden clubs and next to her an Ed Sheeran wannabe tries to get his sensitive songs across. Good luck with that. She cut through Abbeygate Street and crossed back to the west of the river over the Salmon Weir Bridge. Then it was a short walk up University Road. The college buildings were a mix of the old and the new. She made her way to the Arts and Science building and arrived at Professor Leo

Cronin's office at exactly four o'clock. The door was locked so she knocked. There was no answer from within. Ten minutes later she was ready to give up when a middle-aged man rushed along the corridor carrying a briefcase and a pile of papers under his arm.

'Detective Sergeant Fiona Madden?' he asked when he reached her.

Fiona nodded.

'I'm sorry.' He stuck a key in the lock and opened the door. 'I was giving a lecture to the human rights students and I ran over time. Please come in.'

Fiona followed him. He was small and slightly built, bald, and his round face had a ball of fluffy grey hair strategically grown on each cheek. He looked like a character from a Dickens's novel.

He threw his briefcase into the corner of the small room and moved behind an antique, oak partners' desk before flopping into an ergonomic chair that didn't fit with the vibe of the desk. 'I'm bushed. People have the opinion that we university types do nothing but sit around all day cogitating on our specialist subjects. I have a heavy lecture schedule and manage many postgraduate students.'

Fiona sat on a stout wooden chair facing the desk. 'Don't worry, Dr McGoldrick disabused me of that misconception already.'

'Aisling wasn't clear on the purpose of this meeting. She indicated that you were looking for information on the travelling community. Perhaps you could enlighten me on the context.'

'I'm afraid I'm not that clear myself. I'm investigating a series of burglaries in Clifden.' She gave a short description of the crimes. 'My superior suggested it might have something to do with the fact that two traveller families are currently camped in the town for the horse fair.'

'That old chestnut. There's some crime in the area so it

must be the travellers.' He stood and went to a capsule coffee machine on a table behind him. 'Can I offer you a coffee?'

'I'd love one.'

'Colombia okay.'

'Perfect.'

He made two coffees and handed one to Fiona. 'I have no milk or sugar I'm afraid.' He opened a drawer and took out a packet of biscuits.

Fiona waved away the offer of a biscuit.

'You think there's a connection between your break-ins and the travellers in Clifden?'

'It's a hypothesis.' She sipped her coffee. 'This is good.'

'But you have no evidence.'

'Not a shred.'

'How can I help you?'

'I know little or nothing about the travelling community. My colleagues in the force have a stereotypical view. Wherever there are travellers, there's an uptick in crime. I've looked at the statistics.'

Cronin sipped his coffee. 'The same could be said of any minority community who have suffered from social, economic and educational exclusion. In the US, you have a similar set of circumstances for the American Indians and in Australia for the Aborigines. Some people think of the travelling community as a fairly recent phenomenon. But there was some form of travelling community in Ireland from the twelfth century. The exact origin of the community is unknown. They may have been simply itinerants who took to the road through poverty or they may have been a group of craftsmen offering their skills to a wider public. The core problem is that they have developed a series of traditions that are at odds with our current mores.'

'For example?'

'The family feud; most of the violence perpetrated in this country by travellers is associated with grudges held by different groups. The feud has its genesis in the faction fights that took place in Ireland down through the centuries.'

'There's a rumour of a feud between the two families in Clifden. The local station is aware. You're telling me that the general perception that the travellers are synonymous with crime isn't true.'

'No, I'm saying that excluded groups in general are synonymous with crime.'

Fiona drained her coffee cup. She could see the truth in Cronin's remark. 'Two final questions, when I was in Clifden I heard a group of travellers speaking a strange language. I'm a native Gaelic speaker myself and I thought for a minute that it might have been a dialect but I didn't understand a word.'

'Travellers developed their own language. They call it Shelta but some call it Cant or Gammon. It's a mixture of English and Gaelic but many of the words have been inverted. For example, the Irish word for good is maith but in Shelta it becomes taim.' Cronin glanced at his watch. 'I have a meeting with a student in ten minutes. What's your second question?'

'Do travellers claim to have psychic powers?'

'Don't confuse Irish travellers with the Romany or gypsies as we call them. Like the Romany, they may claim to tell the future and they often give readings at fairs. But there's nothing in the literature to suggest that travellers have inbred psychic powers.'

Fiona stood and extended her hand. 'Thanks, you've been extremely helpful.'

Cronin shook. 'Glad to be of assistance. Travellers have a bad rap as the kids say. There are bad apples in every group but collectively I've found them to be decent people.' He produced a card from his desk drawer and handed it to Fiona. 'If you have any more questions concerning travellers, you can contact me.'

She took the card and dropped it into her pocket. 'I will.'

CHAPTER EIGHT

Fiona almost ran into a young female student heading for Cronin's office. She checked her watch. It was almost five o'clock and there was no point in returning to Mill Street. Both Aisling and Cronin were at pains to point out that crime wasn't the preserve of travellers. On the other hand, she was heartened by his opinion that the travellers had no history of being psychics. That had been her sneaky question, the one that had no relation to the crime she was investigating. Maybe she would start sleeping properly at night. But she wasn't sure. Every time she closed her eyes, she could see the face of the old woman at the Connors' camp. Aisling's office was on the second floor of the Arts and Science building and she decided to pass by and pick her up. It was too nice an evening to head home and she fancied a beer somewhere quiet where there was a view of the sea. Her local hostelry, Taaffes, would be out to the door with tourists.

Aisling was engaged with a student and Fiona had to wait in the corridor. Eventually, the door opened and a male student hurried off in the direction of the stairs.

'What did you do to that poor boy?' Fiona closed the door behind her.

'That poor boy had turned in three essays in a row that have been utter tripe. One more and he's going to have to find a new faculty that will put up with his laziness.'

'I thought we might go to Taaffes for a drink or two.'

'What about a bottle of chardonnay in the back garden?'

'You mean, you, me and ten thousand midges, no thanks.'

'Okay.' Aisling gathered the papers on her desk and put them into a file. 'I'm off to Dublin at the weekend.'

'Psychology conference?'

'No, it's my mom and dad's fortieth wedding anniversary.'

'I didn't think that you guys were talking.'

'They've extended an olive branch to me.'

'I don't suppose that the branch is long enough to reach me.'

Aisling picked up her briefcase. 'It's a first step.'

'I should have asked Cronin what he knew about lesbians. I'm sure we deserve the same attention as the travellers.'

As expected, Taaffes was packed to the rafters. Fiona and Aisling had to pick their way through a forest of rucksacks, bodhrans and bazooka cases. The barman, good solid man that he was, winked at Fiona and indicated towards the rear where they found two stools which, by some miracle, were free.

'It pays to be a regular,' Fiona settled herself on her stool and signalled to the barman for drinks for herself and Aisling.

'How did you get on with Leo?'

'I didn't expect to get much of an insight into my crime and that's exactly what I got. He's a nice man but an academic.'

'So, we're all a bunch of useless so-and-sos.'

'That's not what I meant. He sees the travellers as a group of dispossessed and undervalued people and it's his life's work to redress that situation.'

'And you?'

'I visited two camps in Clifden. The caravans are relatively new and the vehicles are brand new. The sites are littered with trash and the adults are sitting around playing cards. I was born in a council house in a tiny village, my father ran off when I was a child and I was raped as a teenager. Nobody helped my mother and no one helped me. You don't have a professor here who writes learned papers on the plight of people who got off their arses and dug themselves out of a hole.'

'Let's agree to disagree.'

Their drinks arrived and Fiona paid. 'Sorry, I'm a bit agitated lately,' she said. 'Horgan handed over the three men we arrested yesterday to another team of detectives. We made the arrest and it should be up to Tracy and me to follow up. It was our collar and it should go on our record. I was the one that put the stolen van and the burglaries together. Horgan has it in for me.'

'Don't be paranoid.'

'There's no other answer.' Fiona sipped her Guinness.

'Is that all that's on your mind?'

'No, that's not all. I'm pissed that the olive branch hasn't been extended to me. I didn't give a damn for the McGoldricks. In fact, I don't know them since I've never met them. Everything I know about them you told me. They're the cliché Irish couple: confession on Saturday evening and Mass and Communion on Sunday morning. Unlike fifty per cent of the population, they didn't reject their religion during the heady days of the economic boom of the early years of the new millennium. They felt vindicated when, after the bust of 2007, those who had left flooded back to the Church for comfort. They haven't slept in the same bed for more than twenty years. The official explanation is that your father snores. Gay sex and the gay lifestyle are an aberration and I'm the harlot that lured their daughter into a life of sin. The McGoldricks and their celebration of their forty years together can go to hell. But I'm still pissed. How did I do?' She knew she was dodging the fact that Peggy's remark about death hovering over her had put her on edge.

'Wow, it proves you listen to me.'

Fiona raised her hand to signal another round but Aisling shook her head. 'The noise in this place is wrecking my head. It's a beautiful evening, there's a fish restaurant in the harbour at Barna. Let's have a meal and see if we can work out why Horgan is being so hard on you.'

CHAPTER NINE

Fiona finally fell asleep on the living room couch at one o'clock. She was in a deep sleep when she heard the phone ring. She dragged herself awake and was searching for the phone when Aisling opened the bedroom door.

'Would you answer that damn thing for God's sake?' Aisling said.

'How come the phone is never on the cradle?' She discarded the remote controls for the TV and the satellite before picking up the phone from the coffee table, pressing the green button and putting it to her ear.

'DS Madden?' the voice on the other end said.

'Speaking.'

'Garda Doyle on the night desk at Mill Street.'

'Is this a joke?' She looked at her watch. Three thirty. Why did everything have to happen in the middle of the night?

'I'm calling for DI Horgan. You and Detective Garda Tracy are to get yourselves to Clifden. One of the guards has found a dead body. I've called Tracy and he's on his way to collect a car. He'll pick you up in twenty minutes.'

The phone went dead in her hand. She staggered to the bathroom, got out of her clothes and stepped into the shower.

. . .

'Probably some guy lying dead drunk in a gutter,' Fiona said as soon as she settled herself into the car's passenger seat.

'Surely they would have checked before calling us out.'

Fiona hated Tracy at this point. Four o'clock in the morning wasn't the time for doing his enthusiastic puppy act. 'You obviously haven't been in the force long enough. A lot of our colleagues cannot recognise the difference between the dead and the dead drunk. And you and I have already been sent on one fool's errand. Hogan is abusing us.' She slipped into silence. Maybe this was what the old woman was talking about.

'Did you get any further details?'

'No, drive us to Clifden and all will be revealed. In the meantime, let me have a little snooze. I'm operating on three hours' sleep.' She leaned her head against the door and closed her eyes.

Two murders in as many months. Fiona knew she was harsh in dealing with Tracy's exuberance. This was the same guy who had puked his guts up at the sight of Sarah Joyce's dead body on the beach at Caladh Mweenish. God only knew what was awaiting them in Clifden. Tracy would soon get his fill of dead bodies and he'd end up praying for a case of bog-standard burglary. She would take good old-fashioned crime over murder any day. At least with a break-in, nobody was going to the mortuary.

They stopped at the station in Clifden. The lights were blazing and it looked like the full complement had been called in. Glennan was in the tea room with some of his officers who looked the worse for wear.

'Tea?' he said as soon as they entered.

'Please,' Fiona said.

Tracy nodded.

'What have we got?' Fiona took a mug of tea that already had milk in it. She sipped it gingerly, used to taking her hot drinks without accompaniment.

'Damned if I know.' Glennan passed a cup to Tracy. 'This place was chock-a-block with people yesterday. It's one of our busiest days of the year. The pubs were out the door last night until well past closing. One of our patrols found the body at just after three and called it in. They initially thought he was drunk so there might be some contamination of the site. They secured the area and you're the first to arrive. The local doctor is indisposed so they're sending someone out from Galway. And they're rousing CSI. Now you know what I know.'

'How much contamination?' Fiona asked.

'I'm not sure.'

'It's okay, CSI will process your men.' She finished her tea. 'Let's go look.'

Glennan dumped his teacup into the sink and followed Fiona and Tracy. 'You can leave the car. The body is only two hundred yards down the road. I was here yesterday and this road was littered with horseboxes and cars. And people. If someone witnessed this crime, and if they don't come forward, we're going to have a hell of a job to find them.' He handed each of them a pair of plastic overshoes.

'The problem is that most of them won't understand what they've seen,' Fiona said. 'And they're the sober ones.'

She and Tracy put on the shoes and took gloves from their pockets.

They walked down the main road into Clifden. The street had been blocked off with crime scene tape and an officer was posted holding a clipboard.

'I'd like to get the road opened by morning,' Glennan said.

'I know,' Fiona said. 'And I'd like to have the murder solved by this afternoon but I suppose neither of us is going to be satisfied.'

Glennan lifted the crime scene tape and Fiona ducked underneath.

She nodded to the guard with the clipboard. 'Detective Garda Tracy will log us in.'

She stopped and looked at the scene. They were on the main road about a hundred and fifty yards from the entrance to the town. There was a garage almost opposite and a hotel beyond that. Behind was a large builder's merchants. There had been no effort to conceal the body.

Fiona and Glennan strode to where two uniformed officers stood.

'Are these the lads that found the body?' Fiona asked.

'Yes, they were on a routine patrol when they noticed the man slumped by the side of the road.'

The corpse was lying on his back in the thick grass just off the edge of the road. He looked asleep except for the pallor of his skin. He could be in his thirties and had a full head of dark hair. He was dressed in a linen jacket over a polo shirt and a pair of light-brown chinos, a pair of black Adidas trainers on his feet. There was no sign of a struggle in the surrounding area and no great amount of blood. Fiona could believe that a passer-by might have believed the dead man to be sleeping it off. She would wait for the doctor to estimate the time of death but she guessed that the man had been dead for more than twelve hours.

She turned to the two guards. 'Is this the way you found him You didn't move him?'

'God, no,' the older of the two said. 'I felt for a pulse was all. He was lying there and we assumed he was drunk but he had a pallor on him and I thought he might be deceased.'

'Did anyone check his pockets?' she asked.

The two uniforms shook their heads.

'Give your names to Detective Garda Tracy. We'll need statements from both of you for the record.'

Fiona knelt beside the body. 'What did you do to get yourself killed?' He would have been a good-looking man when there was a bit of animation in his face. Fiona had viewed many corpses and a lot of them hadn't been in good condition. But to her, they had always looked like wax images of real people. She had never been present when anyone had passed. When her grandmother died, she'd been banished to another room, considered too young to view death and what was in front of her. She'd been told by those that had been present that there is a transition moment when life leaves the body. The eyes of the deceased dimmed and what people called the spirit departed. That was all too religious for her. She stood up. 'I assume he's not a local?'

'Not as far as I know,' Glennan said. 'I know pretty much everyone in town. Of course, he might live in one of the outlying villages.'

'Or he might be a visitor from Mars.'

Glennan smiled. 'Unlikely but possible.'

'Then let's hope he has some identification on him.' She turned to Tracy. 'Get some photos of the scene.'

Tracy took out his mobile and took a series of photos of the body from different angles.

Glennan tapped Fiona on the shoulder. 'Looks like our colleagues from the technical branch have arrived.'

Fiona turned. A van bearing the logo "Garda Technical Branch" was driving in their direction. She watched the van stop. A man and a woman exited and went to the rear. Fiona recognised the man from the beach where Sarah Joyce had been found but she couldn't remember his name.

The two technical branch officers had suited up and were carrying a large box each when they appeared from the rear of the van.

Fiona and Glennan went to meet them.

'DS Madden and Sergeant Glennan, what do you have?' the male technical officer said.

'A corpse,' Glennan said. 'We haven't touched him but it

looks like he didn't die of natural causes. You're Foley. I remember you from Caladh Mweenish.'

'Right, this is my colleague, Marie O'Malley. She's just joined us. I hope we have better luck finding something helpful here.'

Fiona examined O'Malley. They were getting younger every year. O'Malley looked like she'd left school last week. She noticed Tracy giving her the once over. 'Don't you ever give it a rest?'

'We'd better get on with it,' Foley said. 'When is the doctor arriving?'

'The local guy is away so we've given Westdoc a call. He should be here soon. There's a cup of tea at the station when you're finished.'

'Thanks,' Foley said

'I'm going into conference with Sergeant Glennan,' Fiona said. 'Detective Garda Tracy, you stay here and keep the CSIs company.'

CHAPTER TEN

Fiona and Glennan walked away from the crime scene.
'Any ideas?' Fiona asked.

'There was the usual horseplay around town last night but nothing serious.

'What about the burglaries?'

'Nothing, we'll nail them. And if we don't, we can't win them all.'

'That's what we tell ourselves. But our superiors are obsessed with the crime figures and the only word they look for on the file is solved.'

'Some you have to let go. How is Tracy settling in?'

'He's a good copper and someday he might make a good detective. But I think that the boys in the Park have something else in mind for him. He's a graduate and he's going to look the part in a blue uniform covered in gold braid.'

'Lucky for some. It took me twenty years to get my sergeant stripes. And I don't think I'm going any further. But that doesn't bother me. Any ideas on the murdered man?'

'There too little blood about and there was no attempt to hide the body. Also, there wasn't a penny piece in his pockets and no identification that I could find. In fact, his pockets appeared to be empty.'

'Could have been a mugging that went wrong.'

'Maybe, or the killer might be playing silly buggers with us.'

'How so?'

'I don't really know. There are a couple of things that don't gel. I'll wait until the techs report and the doctor gets here.'

'Speak of the devil.' Glennan pointed up the road where a small saloon car was approaching. 'It looks like the doctor has arrived.'

The man who stepped out of the car carrying the obligatory black bag was tall, thin and young. He and O'Malley might have been in the same class in school. Not many doctors were content to live in the middle of nowhere and fill in for local GPs. A travelling doctor's life was for those who couldn't find anything else. Fiona shook hands with the new arrival. He introduced himself as Doctor Gregan. Foley and O'Malley had turned the body over revealing the dark bloodstain on the back of the deceased. A small amount of blood had soaked into the ground beneath the corpse.

Gregan bent and gave the body a cursory examination. He tried to make a meal of it but a dead body on a roadside with a stab mark on his back didn't present much of a challenge.

'What's the story? Fiona asked when he finished his examination

'Stabbed in the back.' Gregan was already packing away his thermometer.

'You don't say,' Fiona said.

'I haven't seen many injuries like it but I'd say that since the knife penetrated the heart, death was instantaneous. The pathologist should be able to confirm.'

'So the man has been stabbed and is dead,' Fiona said. 'Is there anything else you'd like to divulge? Like the time of death, for example.'

'Rigor is well advanced. I've taken his temperature and using the equation I'd guess that he died sometime last night.'

'Nothing more exact than that.' Fiona asked herself what had she been expecting. Gregan was more used to dealing with domestic injuries. 'What makes you think the knife penetrated to the heart.'

'There has been a lot of exsanguination. His clothes are soaked in blood.'

'There doesn't look to be much blood in the surrounding area.'

'There isn't.'

'He wasn't killed here?'

'I don't think so but that's not a medical conclusion. That's for you to establish.' He closed the catch on his satchel. 'You can move him when you're ready. I have a woman in Camus who is well into labour so I'd better be on my way.'

'Thank you.'

He strode off in the direction of the white saloon with the Westdoc logo on the side.

Fiona looked at Glennan. 'Time to call the wagon for our dead friend.'

'We have an ambulance in town. I'll give them a call. Are you going to inform Horgan that we're dealing with a murder?'

'It's too early to bother him with such dreadful news. We'll let him have his breakfast first. Let's see if the technical team have found anything interesting.'

Fiona and Tracy walked to where Foley and O'Malley were standing together beside their van. 'Anything interesting for us?' Fiona asked.

'The place where the body is lying is the equivalent of a ploughed field,' Foley said. 'Yesterday was the horse fair and this area has been churned up by dozens of horses. There may be some evidence but we haven't found it. We've combed the area around the body and bagged everything we found. It's a mixed bag: cigarette butts and drinks cans mainly. We'll sift the bags when we get back to base. We've taken a soil sample around the body but there are dozens of shoe prints. We've taken photos of the prints and the body. I'm going to ask Glennan to cordon off the area in case we need to come back.'

'You didn't stumble across the murder weapon by any chance?'

'If you ever give up the police, you could try your hand as a comedian. On second thoughts, don't bother.'

'Anything in his clothes?'

'He's clean as a whistle.'

'No car keys, bus tickets, room key?'

'Nothing.'

'Do you think he was killed here?'

'I doubt it. Given the position of the body, I'd guess he was killed somewhere else and dumped here.'

Fiona was lost in thought.

'If you find the crime scene,' Foley continued, 'let us know. My report will be with you as soon as possible.'

'We may need it before then,' Fiona said.

'Very funny.' Foley unzipped his suit and threw it into the rear of the van. 'What's the tea like in the station?'

'Over sweetened and already milked.' Fiona watched Tracy unzip O'Malley. It looked like he'd had practice.

'Then I think we'll give it a miss,' Foley said. 'There's a nice café for breakfast in Oughterard.' He leaned in to Fiona. 'You ought to keep an eye on your partner. He's a sexual harassment case waiting to happen.'

'Thanks for the advice.'

'That wasn't very productive,' Tracy said as they watched the van disappear down the road.

'I wouldn't say that. You got to meet O'Malley.'

'I was just helping her out of her gear.'

'You had your hands on her. Don't do it again.'

'That's a bit harsh. She wasn't complaining.'

'She might change her mind or someone might change it

for her. A copper in Dublin was hounded out of the force when his youngest daughter remembered he had assaulted her as a child. She was undergoing regression treatment at the time. Another of his daughters supported her with a similar allegation. The eldest daughter saved him from prison when she rubbished her sister's statements. Just keep your hands to yourself and your dick in your pants. It's safer that way.'

Fiona stood over the body. 'Who are you? How did you get here and where were you staying?'

'Where do we start?' Tracy asked.

'I'm damned if I know. Someone has been damn clever here. Most murderers make at least one mistake that leads to their undoing. They leave a notebook or a mobile phone on the victim that facilitates the police investigation. We have a nameless victim with not a shred of evidence to help us. The murderer wants us wearing a ball and chain to slow us down. I wonder why.'

An ambulance with its hazard lights flashing came towards them.

'There's nothing more we can do here and the boss will have finished his eggs and bacon by now. Before we head back to Galway, I want Glennan to get his lads to comb the area around the body. I don't hold out much hope but you never know.'

'Sounds pretty hopeless.'

The ambulance pulled in beside them and Fiona led Tracy away while the attendants got on with their job.

'Welcome to the wonderful world of murder investigation,' Fiona said.

CHAPTER ELEVEN

'That doesn't sound good.' Horgan flopped back into an empty chair which creaked but didn't collapse. They had been standing at the whiteboard viewing the photos of the corpse that Tracy had printed from his phone while Fiona briefed him on the preliminary examination of the body in Clifden.

She stared at him. 'I suppose you know the meaning of understatement. We have no idea who the victim is, we don't know where he was murdered and we haven't got a murder weapon. And there's no CCTV anywhere near where the corpse was deposited. It looks like the murderer covered all the bases. Could it sound any less good?'

'You're the experienced murder detective,' Horgan said. 'Don't tell me you've never been in a situation like this.'

'I've never been in a situation like this. And it gets worse. There could have been upwards of three thousand non-residents in Clifden yesterday. That's three thousand visitors who packed up their traps and headed off home when their business was concluded. That's three thousand potential suspects that we have no idea who they are. Any one of them could have knifed the victim, put him in the boot of their car and dumped the body before they left town.'

'Maybe we should call the specialists in from Dublin.'

'It may be a coincidence but have you ever seen a film called *Out of Innocence*?'

'I don't think so.'

'I saw it a few weeks ago on television. It's about how the murder squad from Dublin made a hash of the Kerry babies' investigation. Everybody ended up with shit on their faces, including the commissioner. Do you want to be the one who calls them in?'

'Maybe the Park will insist.'

'Not if they were watching the film.'

'How do you suggest we progress?'

'Right now, we don't have any evidence to work with so we have to find some. I don't know where I read it but someone a lot smarter than me suggested that there was no such thing as the perfect crime. That means that there is evidence out there. The uniforms will search the area where the body was found. They may turn up something relevant.' She didn't want to say that the chances were not good.

Tracy entered the squad room carrying a tray containing two takeaway coffee cups and a carrier bag. He handed Fiona a coffee and a Danish pastry.

Fiona bit into the pastry, chewed, and washed it down with a mouthful of coffee. 'Late breakfast,' she explained to Horgan. 'We didn't have time for the eggs, rashers and toast after being called out at four o'clock.'

'My heart bleeds for you,' Horgan said.

Fiona said. 'I wonder, was one of the state broadcasting vans in the vicinity?'

'There was a report on the horse fair on the evening news,' Tracy said. 'There was a TG4 film crew covering the event.'

Fiona smiled. 'And I suppose there were a lot of people

with their mobile phones out taking photos and video of the horses.'

'It goes with the territory,' Tracy said.

'We need to get our hands on every piece of film from the horse fair that we can.' She looked at Tracy. 'You can start with TG4. Get a copy of whatever they shot in Clifden yesterday.'

'That's a bit of a shot in the dark,' Tracy said. 'What's the chance that the dead man was even in Clifden during the time TG4 were filming.'

'It's a start,' Fiona said. 'The post-mortem is being carried out this afternoon.'

'I received a call from the state pathologist's office,' Horgan said. 'They've passed the post-mortem to a local quack at the regional hospital.'

'It's Galway University Hospital,' Tracy said.

'The locals call it the regional,' Fiona said before Horgan could intervene. She would have to warn Tracy not to continually correct a superior.

Horgan's phone rang. He stood up and walked out of earshot to take the call.

Fiona and Tracy concentrated on their breakfast while he was gone.

'That was the chief super,' Horgan said on his return. 'I included the dead body on his morning brief. He's already had a call from the Connaught Tribune and a TG4 van has been dispatched.' He looked at Fiona. 'Raidió na Gaeltachta want a comment from a native speaker for their news segment and, unfortunately, you're the chosen one. Keep it simple, and short.'

Fiona nodded. 'I know the story, early days of the investigation, waiting on the results of the post-mortem before we decide on the direction of our enquiries.'

Horgan held up his phone. A local number was displayed. 'Call this number for the interview. Do it as soon as you can.'

'I'll ask the listeners to send us their photos taken at the horse fair.'

'Keep me informed.' Horgan headed back to his office.

'What do we do now?' Tracy asked.

'Get the footage from yesterday. There'll probably be lots of crowd scenes so you're likely to need facial recognition software. With a bit of luck, we'll find a few shots of the victim.'

'Is there a reason why I get all the fun jobs?'

'Don't worry, you'll be out of the trenches shortly. I'm tired of hearing that you're going to be my future boss. In the meantime, you'll do whatever you're asked to do. And you'll smile while you're doing it.'

CHAPTER TWELVE

Tracy was doing his best to fight off the tiredness but he was losing the battle. He'd had three hours' sleep and his tank of energy was running on empty. He envied the people who could have a quick catnap and recharge the batteries in a matter of hours. There was the possibility of asking for a few hours off to catch up on his sleep but that would show weakness. Fiona was out there somewhere pursuing the case. He was getting a little pissed off with all the talk of the glittering career ahead. Graduates were few and far between in the force which had an anti-intellectual ethos. His colleagues were generally big lads who could handle themselves and weren't fazed by standing in the middle of a road checking the tax and insurance of cars. One day of that type of duty and he would be ready to eat his own head. He'd managed to pass out of the police college at Templemore at the head of his class and he knew that the fact had not escaped his superiors. So, there had been no scut duty for Garda Tracy. He had been obliged to spend three years in a squad car in Cork before being tipped the wink that he should apply for CID and his detective's badge. There was truth in the rumour that he was being fast-tracked but he didn't like the fact that the rumour had spread so widely. He picked up his sixth cup of coffee and drained it. Several of his classmates at Templemore were still in contact and their congratulatory emails on the appearance of his name in the papers in relation to the solving of the Sarah Joyce murder had dripped with envy. His head was falling forward when the sound of his phone jerked him upright.

'Cliona Gallagher *anseo, an féider liom labhairt le Garda Tracy.*'

Tracy quickly cleared the fog from his mind. He had contacted TG4, the Irish-speaking television station, and been passed on to the producer responsible for the shoot at the horse fair. From there he had been given the contact of the freelance camera operator who still had the tapes in her possession. He'd called her and left a message. He didn't remember her name but this had to be her.

'Detective Garda Sean Tracy, I'm sorry I speak a certain amount of Gaelic but I'm more comfortable in English. Do you mind?'

'English is fine but you should practice a bit now that you're in Galway. I got your message but I was busy on a shoot. How can I help you?'

'I spoke to a producer at TG4. You were in charge of the camera or their shoot in Clifden yesterday.' She had a soft northern accent that Tracy thought might be from Donegal. She sounded young.

'I was.'

'I don't know if you've heard the news but a man was found murdered in Clifden this morning. We're looking for anyone who might have been with him at the fair and we were wondering if we might look at the footage you shot yesterday.'

'Sure, I have a couple of hours of tape. I could put it on a CD for you and you could review it on your computer.'

'Where are you located and I'll drop by to collect it?'

'I'm at my office in Galway.' She gave him an address ten minutes away.

'How long will it take to copy the tape?'

'Give me ten minutes.'

'I'll be there in ten, and thanks for returning the call.'

'Always happy to help the law.'

Tracy hung up. He felt a jolt of energy but was worried whether it would last. He put on his jacket and left the office.

THE BRASS PLATE outside the address Tracy had been given said 'Aesop Productions' and he assumed that Gallagher was an employee. He pushed the bell and waited. The door was opened by a young woman with the most astonishing head of red hair that he'd ever seen. Her face was pale in comparison but her features were perfect. Tracy tended to fall in love at first sight and if this was Cliona Gallagher, she put every other woman out of his mind.

'You're Tracy?'

'Sean, please, do you need to see my warrant card?'

'No, I've got your tape.'

'I love that soft northern accent. You're from Donegal.' Tracy's fatigue was a thing of the past. He stood up straight.

'Yes, you really are a detective.' She made no attempt to invite him inside. 'Wait here, I'll get it for you.'

She returned and handed him a CD in a plastic sleeve.

'Thanks, this could be helpful.'

She made to close the door.

'You've been really great about this. I'm just about to go for a late lunch and I hate eating alone.'

'I bet you say that to all the girls.'

'Not really. I'm new in Galway and I haven't made many friends. In my experience, people tend to be wary of us coppers.'

She looked at her watch. 'I've never lunched with a Garda

or a detective before and life is about experiences. I'll get my jacket.'

Tracy felt a warm glow. This could be the one.

CHAPTER THIRTEEN

'Surely you don't mean to consume everything that's on that plate?' Aisling was staring at the mixed grill that Fiona had ordered. They were sitting in the Charcoal Grill on Prospect Hill.

'I'm starving,' Fiona said through a mouthful of spiced sausage. 'Getting woken up at four o'clock in the morning to view a dead body gives me the appetite of a horse.' She looked at Aisling's plate. 'What do you call that gunk again?'

'Mezze, it's a mixture of Turkish starters. You don't have much to go on with your new case.'

'It's rare to have a murder where there is a distinct absence of evidence. Either the criminals are getting smarter or the police are getting dumber.' She pointed at Aisling with her knife. 'Don't answer that.'

'It is relatively unheard of to come across someone who doesn't have a scrap of identification on him.'

'It's also unheard of to have someone whose pockets are completely empty. This man didn't have a cent on him, no credit cards, no car keys, no bus stub. Someone wants us to work for our corn. The general public thinks that the police solve most murders but that's an illusion that the newspapers present. The truth is that there are a total of 840 missing persons in Ireland and about nine thousand people are reported missing each year. I think the oldest case still open dates from 1951.' She didn't add that her rapist was one of the missing. 'There has to be a certain number of the missing who are buried under the pear tree. In other words, there may be many murder victims out there who have never been found. Given the lack of evidence in my current case, I wouldn't be surprised if he ends up in the cold case file.'

'Nobody passes through this world unnoticed. Your victim may have a wife and children, parents who love him, siblings. He'll be on a government database somewhere. You have his likeness surely that is a sound place to start.'

Fiona pushed her plate away. She had managed to get through seventy per cent of the meat-laden dish but she could go no further. 'I should have lunch with you more often. You've got me thinking. Why was his body dumped where someone could easily come across it? There are a million bog holes in the vicinity of Clifden where he could have been deposited and we'd have been none the wiser. It looks like someone wanted him found. But why?'

'The murderer didn't have time to dispose of the body. He might not have been familiar with the area and know the location of a suitable bog hole.'

'Or it was a message. We always find the bodies from the drug hits and the gang turf wars. The killers want the other side to know that they're serious.'

'Coffees and the bill?'

'Yeah, I need to get back to work. There's a post-mortem I need to attend and you need to get back to this great book you're writing. I bet James Patterson is shaking in his boots.'

Aisling waved at the waitress. 'Don't be facetious. You know full well that it's a textbook on the treatment of autistic children. It'll cost a fortune and I suppose it'll sell a few dozen copies. I'm not doing it to make money but to assist practitioners.'

'And be invited to speak at conferences located in nice places with all expenses paid.'

'You really are a detective.' The waitress arrived and Aisling asked for the coffees and the bill. 'Don't forget I'll be away for the weekend.'

'Oh yes, the big family gathering. The prodigal daughter is welcomed back into the bosom of the family that threw her out so recently. The reconciliation of the McGurk family. The sexual deviant returns.'

'I knew you'd react like this.'

'Then why did you bloody tell me.'

'Because I want our relationship to be honest. I think there might be something else about my potential reconciliation with my family that bothers you.'

'And what would that be?'

'You have one close family member that you haven't spoken to in eighteen years. Perhaps my trip to Dublin has opened that wound again. Your mother lives sixty kilometres away. She's getting old and is probably lonely. I know you blame her for what happened with your son but it was a different time and you weren't the only young girl in this country who was treated harshly by the combination of the Church and the State. There are others who suffered much worse indignities and who carry the scars. Your mother isn't a monster. She was just another manipulated female.'

Fiona finished her coffee. 'I hope you enjoy your trip to Dublin and I'll be interested to learn the result. But don't think that there's any comparison in our situations. You followed your nature. I was the victim of a crime that had consequences. I love you and I want to be your partner but you're going to have to stop psychoanalysing me.' She stood. 'Lunch is on you.'

CHAPTER FOURTEEN

Fiona arrived at the appointed hour for the post-mortem to find that the procedure had been completed and the pathologist from Galway University Hospital had returned to her office. She made her way to the consulting room and knocked on Professor Claire Daly's office door.

'Come in.' The tone was sharp and businesslike.

Fiona entered the office. 'Professor Daly?'

'No, I'm her secretary.' The woman who sat behind the desk spoke with a clipped English accent. 'Do you have an appointment?'

Fiona removed her warrant card from her pocket. 'No, not for another forty years or so I hope. I didn't know that pathologists took patients.' She held the open warrant card a foot from the secretary's face. 'Detective Fiona Madden, I came to attend the post-mortem of the man found murdered in Clifden.'

'I see, please take a seat and I'll see if the professor is free.'

Fiona sat and watched the secretary use her handset to call her boss. She noticed a door to the side of the secretary's desk and assumed it led to an inner office. The secretary adopted her reverential tone for her boss and announced Fiona's arrival.

'She's on the phone but will be with you presently.'

Fiona sat in an alcove, picked up a copy of Conde Nast's *Traveller* magazine from the coffee table and examined the cover. The articles highlighted places she could only dream of visiting. It had been her experience that the magazines provided on the tables of medical waiting rooms said a lot about the leisure activities of the practitioner. The golfer would have dog-eared copies of *Golf Monthly* while the fishing nut might have old copies of *Field and Stream*. What did *Traveller* magazine say about Professor Daly? That she had plenty of money and liked exotic travel.

'The professor will see you now.'

Fiona came out of her reverie and looked at the secretary who nodded in the direction of the door.

'Professor Daly?' Fiona said as she entered the room.

'DS Madden.' Daly looked up from a file she was examining. She was in her early forties with dark hair cut short. Her face was round and the lines around her eyes said that she liked to smile often. Fiona noticed two silver frames on the desk and the wall behind had a series of framed diplomas prominently displayed and facing the visitor. Most of the diplomas had been awarded by the University of British Columbia in Vancouver. 'What can I do for you?'

'I was hoping to attend the post-mortem of the murder victim that was brought in this morning. The information I received indicated that it was scheduled for this afternoon at two thirty.'

'Please take a seat.'

Fiona sat on a chair facing Daly. She couldn't place the accent but she assumed that it was Canadian mixed with something.

'I was told from Dublin that the post-mortem was urgent so I moved it up and did it over my lunch break. I already had a busy afternoon and I didn't want to be rushing around like a blue-arsed fly.'

Fiona had never examined a fly's ass so maybe all the flies in Canada had blue asses.

'I wish I had been informed.'

'It was pretty straightforward. There was no point in ruining your lunch.'

'Anything I should know?'

'It'll all be in the report.'

'We don't have a lot of evidence and we're under a certain amount of time pressure. If there is something in the post-mortem that might give us a lead, I'd like to know about it now. Also, I'd like a copy of the photos that were taken during the procedure.'

'I'm sorry, I should have informed you of the change. The victim was in his mid-thirties and was in robust good health despite a slightly enlarged liver. My guess is that he was a heavy drinker from an early age. I don't think that he worked with his hands. I scraped under his fingernails but they were chewed to the butt. I bagged the little I found and sent it to the forensic lab. I think he had many years of life before him. The cause of death was clear: a knife wound to the heart. Whoever did it knew what they were doing. The strike was perfect and death would have been instantaneous. From the direction of the wound, I would say that he was stabbed from behind and the murderer was left-handed or at least used his left hand. The knife would have been at least six to eight inches long with a sharp point. If you asked me to guess what kind of knife we're talking about, I'd say it was a common kitchen knife.'

'Not the kind of knife one tends to carry around in one's pocket.'

'I don't think so. There were a number of bruises on the torso that were made antemortem.'

'Would there have been much blood?'

'Buckets.'

'We have no idea who the victim was. There was nothing, and I mean nothing, on the body. Were there any distinguishing marks on the body?'

'There were several scars but most of them were old. His left sleeve was tattooed from wrist to elbow but the shape was geometric.'

'No lettering at all?'

Daly shook her head. 'The lab is examining his stomach contents but I found traces of meat and bread, vegetables and alcohol. My guess would be a burger, salad, chips and a Guinness.'

'He was at the horse fair.'

'That could account for the contents.'

'What about time of death?'

'The corpse was left in the open during the night so that complicates matters a bit. Sometime between ten and midnight is the best that I can do.'

'Did you X-ray the corpse?'

'I told the assistant to take care of that after I left.'

'And that's it?'

'I'm afraid so. I'd like to tell you that he had his name and address tattooed on his butt, but he hasn't. I'll have the photos on the wire within the hour and you'll have the report tomorrow.'

'Thanks.' Fiona tried to hide her disappointment. There didn't seem to be any light at the end of the tunnel. She stood and extended her hand. 'What made you leave Vancouver for Galway?'

Daly took her hand. 'I loved Vancouver but after I graduated, I joined MSF and toured a bit. That's where I met my husband and as they say, the rest is history. Nice to have met you, Fiona. Good luck with your case.'

CHAPTER FIFTEEN

When Fiona returned to the station, Tracy was examining what looked like the footage from Clifden on his computer. 'You're looking very chipper. When I left before lunch, you looked like something the cat dragged in. I suppose you slipped off home for a kip during lunch.'

'No, I got what might be called a second wind.'

Fiona frowned. 'Is that the TG4 footage from Clifden?'

'Yep, I linked up with the camera operator and got the tape transferred to a CD.'

'Most people would have said cameraman but you said camera operator. I assume the operator was a woman.'

Tracy rubbed his forehead with his left hand. That was his 'tell' when he was embarrassed. 'Yes, Cliona Gallagher.'

'And she's young and good-looking. And that spot of sauce wasn't on your shirt before lunch. So you ate in a restaurant. Did you and Miss Gallagher lunch together?'

'Yes. Enough of the Sherlock Holmes impersonation. She did us a big favour and I invited her to lunch.'

'And somehow you got a second wind. I suppose Maggie Connors is no longer in the picture.'

'Where have you been? I thought you were supposed to be attending the post-mortem.'

'The pathologist started without me. She was finished by the time I arrived. I don't think it makes much difference. There was nothing to learn. He consumed a meal of a meat, salad and chips and probably a pint or glass of Guinness. How did he pay for it if he had no money in his pocket?'

'Maybe he had the exact change, like on the buses.'

'Unlike you, I haven't got my second wind. I'm tired and frustrated that we have no evidence. I did the piece on the phone for Raidió na Gaeltachta and put in a request for anyone who has a relative that didn't come home from the fair or a worker that didn't turn up this morning to contact us. That should draw some response. Whether it leads to anything is another question. How much footage did you get?'

'About two hours. The item on TV lasted two minutes including an interview with one of the organisers. Cliona was paid for the afternoon so she decided to continue filming.'

'Anything so far?'

'Lots of horses' arses but no sign of our man. There are plenty of crowd scenes that I'll have to look at more closely.'

'What about the facial recognition software?'

'I've requested a download. They're looking into it.'

'Why do I sense some hesitancy?'

'I've never used it.'

'Then you'll learn. We need a break. Any kind of a break. This guy was stabbed in the heart. He bled like a stuck pig. Somewhere in the vicinity of Clifden there's a pool of blood you could probably swim in. Any word from Glennan?'

'No.'

She picked up the phone and dialled.

'Glennan.' His voice sounded tired.

'Fiona, how has your day been?'

'Busy, what's the story? I heard your piece on the radio. You've got great Irish.'

Fiona filled him in on the post-mortem and the footage from the TV station. 'How about your end? Anything from the search?'

'The only blood we found was directly beneath the body and it doesn't correspond with what you said about the wound bleeding profusely.'

'We know he wasn't killed where we found him. The killer didn't toss the knife?'

'My lads found nothing, as in zip, nada. Get us a photo of the guy and we'll pin them up around the town. Someone may have seen him about.'

'I'll get Tracy on it.' She looked at the mail on her computer and saw that the post-mortem photos had arrived. 'Anything else to report?'

'There was an altercation this afternoon between the Fureys and the Connors. I have two of the participants charged with disturbing the peace.'

'Which two?'

'Phil Connors and Ted Furey.'

'Are you going to hold them?'

'What do you think?'

'I'd prefer if they didn't move on yet.'

'That can be arranged.'

'I was thinking of moving the incident room to Clifden.'

'We're a bit cramped but I suppose we could find you a room.'

'Thanks, I'll let you know. Go home and get some sleep. It's been a long day.'

'You too.' The line went dead.

Tracy looked up from his computer. 'Any news from Glennan?'

'His boys searched the area but found nothing. It's what I expected. The body was dumped, probably in the middle of the night. Glennan heard me on the radio and so did most of the residents in the area. The local news programme is compulsory listening because it is so local. There's still a chance that somebody saw the drop but didn't realise what they were seeing. It most likely looked like someone depositing a drunk friend. What about the footage?'

'Nothing so far. We seem to be grasping at straws.' He rubbed his eyes. 'I'm so bushed I'm seeing double.'

Fiona looked at the clock. It was ten minutes to six. 'Why don't we call it a day?'

'What about that first forty-eight hours shit? We've already eaten up fourteen and that leaves us thirty-four to identify a suspect. We're out of our depth. Maybe you should let Horgan call in a team from Dublin.'

'And what would they do? We're following the only lines, or should I say line, of enquiry. Our only hope is to find his face on your new girlfriend's footage.'

'She's not my new girlfriend.'

'Are you meeting her tonight? No, you're too tired. The next date is tomorrow night.'

He switched off his computer. 'I could learn to hate you.'

'What about Instagram? There were lots of people there yesterday taking photos. Is it possible to trawl Instagram and Facebook for pictures uploaded from the fair?'

'I suppose.'

Fiona picked up her bag and headed for the door. 'We'll start again tomorrow morning.'

'It's going to be another long day.'

CHAPTER SIXTEEN

Fiona was on her way out of the station when she realised that she had been picked up by Tracy that morning and consequently she had no transport. She considered the alternatives; she could catch a bus or she could walk. The bus was so infrequent that she would be better off walking. Barna was seven and a half kilometres from Galway and it was a fine summer's evening. That would mean a good hour and a half. Normally, she would have been up for it but it had been a long day. However. a brisk walk of that length would be the perfect way to prepare for a nice long shower and a cold glass of wine. She headed east on Mill Street towards Nun's Island. Although the day had been tiring, she took deep breaths and felt invigorated as she made her way through the narrow, cobbled streets heading for the coast at Salthill. It was only when she was forced to commune intimately with the city by walking its streets that she realised how much she loved Galway city and south Connemara. When she'd left after the birth of her son, she'd sworn never to return. Her plan had been to leave her past behind and get away from Ireland completely. She'd considered New Zealand and Australia but didn't have the necessary skills and her research of the visa situation convinced her that she would have to establish herself in a career first before escaping. That led to becoming a police cadet and passing out as a fully-fledged police officer. In time the dream of an escape to the Antipodes faded. In many ways she was glad that it had. The smell of the sea hit her nostrils when she reached the Upper Salthill Road. She walked along the promenade allowing her mind to wander. Becoming a police detective had been her dream job. But reality usually falls short. In Dublin, she had witnessed life at its most venal and destructive. The mixture of greed and immorality had cut deeply into the Irish myth of the country of a hundred thousand welcomes. She glanced out to sea and the world appeared pristine. But beneath the beautiful views, the cities and towns were being corrupted by drugs. A recent survey had shown that many of her colleagues suffered from mental illness. Mostly after viewing murder victims. At the end of the promenade, she turned onto the Barna Road that ran parallel to the sea. She thought about her current murder case. They were somewhere away from looking at issues of motive. Their number one priority was to put a name on the victim and there was little doubt that the murderer wanted to delay that process. The removal of every vestige of identity from the corpse was significant. They had circulated a picture and the description of the victim and they would have to wait and see what came in. She put the work problem to the back of her mind as she passed Galway Bay Golf Club and she concentrated on enjoying the beauty of the walk. Out to sea, she could just see the humps of the Aran Islands visible through a light mist. She promised herself to visit the islands soon. She was walking briskly when she saw the village of Barna straight ahead.

CHAPTER SEVENTEEN

Fiona switched off her bike, locked it and entered the station. She ignored the theatrical look of amazement on the face of the desk sergeant and made her way to the empty squad room. The wall clock said ten past six and she had no idea what she was doing there. Experience told her that nothing had changed overnight. But the desire to push the investigation forward was undeniable. Sleep had evaded her. After the walk from Galway, she'd enjoyed a shower and joined Aisling for a drink before a dinner of fresh hake and salad. There was no discussion of her case or Aisling's impending visit to Dublin and they retired early. She woke at half past one and was instantly awake. Her first thought was that Tracy had been right, time was against them. The first forty-eight hours were important and that was why their canny murderer had stripped the victim of all identification. They were eating up time trying to identify the murdered man. The longer they spent on identifying him the more time the murderer would have to cover up his part in the crime. She'd gone to the kitchen and made herself a cup of herbal tea. There was no way she could see to break the cycle. In order to look for a possible motive for the murder, they would have to examine the victim's life. And to examine his life they would have to know who he was. Motive would have to wait. By the time she had finished her tea, she knew that there was no possibility of returning to sleep. She waited until early morning before heading into the station and now that she was there, she was at a loose end. The murder had featured on the late news. There were pictures of the site where the body had been found and of Glennan's boys carrying out a search of the area. She wouldn't have been the only interested party viewing the footage. Horgan would be put under the gun first thing this morning and that pressure would be passed to her. Maybe it would be best for all concerned to let a squad from Dublin take control of the investigation. She wouldn't like it and neither would her chief super. It wouldn't happen in the short term. But they wouldn't give her a lot of time to produce results. First things first. She opened the file of the investigation and stared at the picture of the corpse. Who the hell are you? Unfortunately, the photo didn't answer. She closed the file, opened her computer and checked her emails. Tracy had put the fingerprints through the system and the victim wasn't in their database. It had been worth a try but it hadn't come off. She'd had two responses to her radio appeal that had come to nothing. The missing men had turned up later most likely having slept it off somewhere. She opened the file again and spread the photos out on her desk. No name and no identifying features. Where could she go next?

She came awake with a start and found herself lying across her desk. The wall clock said eight thirty and her nose twitched at the smell of coffee.

'Here.' Tracy put a cup on her desk as she sat upright. 'Have you been here all night?'

She sipped the hot coffee. 'No, I couldn't sleep so I came in early. I was looking for something in the photos and I must have fallen asleep. Is there any sign of Horgan?'

'Not so far. We were on the box last night. Or at least Glennan was.'

'I saw it: *The victim has yet to be identified.*'

'We drew a zero on the fingerprints.'

'We need to go wider. Let's try Interpol.'

'Don't we have to follow some procedure or other for that?'

'As soon as you've finished your coffee.'

She was halfway through her coffee when her phone rang.

'Good morning.' She recognised Glennan's voice.

'I suppose you saw yourself on TV last night.'

'My kids taped it. Next thing you know I'll be on *Dancing with the Stars*.'

'You looked good. What's the news?' She motioned to Tracy and put the call on speaker.

'Two pieces of news: we've discovered a burned-out car and we caught the burglars red-handed.'

Her mind was racing. 'Where was the burned-out car?'

'On a stretch of bogland ten kilometres outside town. There isn't a house anywhere around and it was only found because the owner of the bog went out last night to cut some turf. Are you thinking what I'm thinking?'

'The car belongs to our victim.'

'Then you are thinking what I'm thinking. The lads tell me that whoever did it knows their business. There's nothing left but the shell, and the registration plates have been removed. I've posted a man on it and asked the technical bureau to examine it. I should warn you that we often find old wrecks dumped in the bogs.'

'But it's worth a look. What about the burglars?'

'Two local twelve-year-old lads. They're well known and were moving up the criminal tree.'

'Nothing to do with the travellers?'

'No, but the antisocial stuff still stands.'

'That whole charade was in vain.'

'Not entirely. Except for the two tribal elders butting

horns, the town has been quieter than usual. It could be down to your visit.'

'But you don't really think that?'

'No, I don't.'

'I'll pick you up on the way.'

'See you in about an hour.' Glennan ended the call.

'We're off to Clifden again.' Tracy didn't look enthusiastic.

'Afraid you'll run into your former flame.'

'Leave it off.'

'Relax, you're not going to Clifden. You're going to stay here and find the procedure for asking our colleagues across the water to run those fingerprints through the National Crime Agency database. While you're doing that, you're going to finish looking at your new friend's footage of the horse fair. And don't forget, I want you to check Facebook and Instagram to see if people are uploading photos of the event. I want the name of anyone who is putting photos on and you'll email them for all of their photos.'

'Is there anything else I should be doing at the same time?'

'I'm sure there is and if I think of it, I'll give you a call.' She dropped the murder file into her bag, put on her jacket and was about to switch off her computer when she heard her surname being shouted from the doorway. She turned and saw her boss. He lifted his right hand and extended his index finger upwards. It was the expected call from above.

CHAPTER EIGHTEEN

Chief Superintendent Charles O'Reilly had an office on the top floor of the station. Fiona seldom interfaced with her superior's superior because both she and O'Reilly liked it that way. When she was summoned to the holy of holies, it meant that there was shit flying in the air. She entered the office directly behind Horgan whose broad back concealed her for a moment. The super's office was nearly as large as the CID squad room and at one end O'Reilly sat behind a large antique partner's desk that was rumoured to be his personal property. On the wall directly behind the desk was a large photo of O'Reilly shaking hands with the president of the republic who, as O'Reilly constantly informed visitors, was a close friend. At the other end of the office, was a fine oak meeting table and six chairs which were the property of Garda Síochána. It was towards the table that O'Reilly's finger was pointing when she came out from behind Horgan's back.

Fiona and Horgan sat together on the right side of the table while O'Reilly lowered himself into a large chair at the head.

'I had a call from the commissioner this morning,' O'Reilly began. 'He was visiting Templemore yesterday and he only learned of the murder victim in Clifden on the television news. His personal assistant is probably cleaning the toilets at the Phoenix Park with a toothbrush as we speak. He wants to know where we stand.' He looked directly at Fiona.

She took out her file and laid the photos on the desk while she ran through the events of the previous morning. She continued with a description of the result of the post-mortem and the obtaining of the footage shot by the television crew. The victim's fingerprints had proved useless thus far since he wasn't on the Garda database. She concluded with the fact that two appeals had been made, one by herself on local radio and one on the television news.

O'Reilly carefully examined the photos and took notes while she spoke. 'We still don't know who the victim is?'

'No, sir,' Horgan said. 'The appeals have turned up nothing new.'

'When I received your summons,' Fiona said, 'I was on my way to Clifden. The local Garda have discovered a burned-out car on a bog close to the town. It probably wouldn't have been found for weeks except the owner of the bog decided that it was a good day to cut turf. The technical bureau has been advised. The car might throw up a lead.'

'The commissioner wondered whether we might need some assistance.' O'Reilly looked from Horgan to Fiona.

'That would be your decision entirely,' Horgan said.

'Absolutely,' Fiona said. 'But as I've already pointed out to DI Horgan, bringing in the heavy mob from Dublin didn't work out so well in the Kerry babies case. We know the local scene and many of the local characters. I don't see where assistance from Dublin might have helped us to date. There will be lots of checking to do once we identify the victim so perhaps DI Horgan might assign a detective or two to assist.'

'I take your point, detective sergeant.' O'Reilly looked at his watch. 'The commissioner is calling back in ten minutes. It's my view that we're doing everything humanly possible to identify the victim. I'll reject assistance from Dublin but I'll revisit that decision as the investigation evolves.' He turned to Horgan. 'Look at your resources and see what you can spare. As long as it doesn't affect the overtime budget.' He stood and returned to his desk.

Horgan and Fiona looked at each other before standing and leaving the room together.

'It's nice to know that your work is appreciated,' Fiona said when they were outside the office. 'I don't think the super has attended his leadership seminar yet.'

'He didn't get where he is because of his leadership skills.'

'How did he get where he is?'

'His father played football for Kerry and won an All-Ireland.'

'As Louis Armstrong sang, it's a wonderful world.'

'Get off to Clifden and for God's sake find out who that poor unfortunate man was.'

CHAPTER NINETEEN

Tracy made one more shot at joining Fiona before she left but he was going to be tied to the office for the day. He made no attempt to hide his disappointment before turning on his computer and bringing up the footage shot by Cliona Gallagher. He was anxious to see her again. It was a shame he'd been so tired yesterday but the risk of falling asleep on a first date was too great. His earlier conversation with Fiona was another example of why he felt he was an open book to her. She had got it so right it frightened him. Cliona had banished all thoughts of Maggie Connors. He wasn't some love-struck teenager with a body full of raging hormones. Maggie Connors was a married woman with a family and he'd been lusting after her. Was he out of his mind? A copy of the facial recognition software had been sent to him but he had no idea how to use it. Computers weren't his 'thing'. He had owned one at college and had learned to use word processing, spreadsheets and graphing but he'd never played games or interacted with the machine. He'd put in a request for a quick course from one of the computer nerds and his request was being considered. The approval would probably arrive sometime after his retirement. He popped the USB containing the footage shot in Clifden into the computer and ran the film to the spot where he had stopped the previous day before moving forward. He stared at the faces in the crowd scenes. There was a photo of the victim on the desk in front of him and he looked at it every few minutes to keep it fresh in his memory. He'd already sent the fingerprints to the UK National Crime Agency and he wondered how long it would take them to get around to them.

He was already bug-eyed from staring at the faces. This wasn't the work that he'd signed up for. During their phone calls, his mother had two refrains: when are you going to get married and produce a grandchild and why are you wasting your education working for the Garda Síochána? She needn't worry. He was asking himself the very same questions. She insisted he was getting long-in-the-tooth. At twenty-five, he was already over the hill. He stopped the film and went back two frames. It was only a side view and it was at the rear of the frame but he was sure it was their man. He zoomed in on the face. The man appeared to be staring at something or someone in front of him. Tracy moved ahead one frame at a time. The camera was panning the crowd and the image of the man moved from left to right of the screen. He examined the people around him. Nothing jumped out at him. He went back to the normal size and looked at the time stamp: ten minutes past three. The victim had been in Clifden during the day but he appeared to be there alone. Tracy took a series of screenshots and printed them off. Perhaps they might be useful although he couldn't think how. He went back to scrolling through the tape.

CHAPTER TWENTY

Fiona relaxed on the drive into Connemara and allowed her mind to wander. Tracy had made his feelings obvious about being left to do the donkey work at the station. She would have preferred to have him along to examine the car but time was advancing and it was necessary to divide their forces to identify the victim though she was sure that she had made the right call on the additional resources from Dublin. It was her experience that the more bodies you threw at a murder investigation the better the chance of a result. But this was the west of Ireland, a sparsely populated rural landscape that had no need for CCTV cameras. Glennan's lads had already canvassed the town and her interview on the radio would have been heard by the locals. The news of an unidentified dead body being found in the locality would be the prime subject of discussion in every pub, café, hairdressers and shop. Speculation would centre on the identity of the dead man and the manner of his death. Given the age profile of the inhabitants which leaned heavily in the direction of the elderly, death was an everyday occurrence. But murder wasn't. If the victim were local, a name would already be circulating. The fact that the door-to-door and the public appeal had drawn a blank meant that it was ninety-five per cent certain that the victim was a stranger. Unfortunately, he wasn't the only stranger in Clifden that day. Which meant they might have to canvas more widely. She was already considering having an artist's sketch made and broadcasting an appeal on *Crime Watch,* a national television programme. The investigation was going nowhere until they removed the first obstacle. She had been ruminating so much on the murder in Clifden that she had been driving by autopilot and she found that she had diverted from the direct route and was travelling towards her home village of Glenmore. Aisling's exhortations for her to reconcile with her mother had somehow displaced her concentration on her work issues. She entered Glenmore, passed the school and thought about the Canavans. Their case was proceeding through the justice system and she had kept well out of it. She drove through the village and stopped beside her mother's house. She switched off the car. Perhaps it was time to put the past to rest. The hurt was still there but the rawness was gone. She'd listened on the radio to the stories of the residents of the mother and baby homes and although she had been treated badly, it was nothing in comparison. The issue of the treatment of young unmarried pregnant girls and their babies had only infringed on the national psyche in recent years. Perhaps her mother had been as much a victim as she had. When she turned and looked at the house, she saw a curtain move and knew her mother was watching. Not today, she thought. She started the car and moved away.

GLENNAN WAS WAITING outside the station when she pulled in. He dropped the cigarette he was smoking and crushed it underfoot before taking his place in the passenger seat.

'Anything new?' Fiona put the car in gear and moved off.

'Not on my side.'

'Those things will kill you.' Fiona passed the site where the body had been found.

'Something kills everybody eventually.'

'But you don't have to help. Where am I going?'

'Turn right at the petrol station and head out the Sky Road. I'll tell you when to turn off.'

Fiona made the right turn. 'What do you think?'

'The locals have a habit of bringing clapped-out cars to the bog to die. They use them as somewhere to get out of the rain if they get caught out. But they're not usually burned out. My lads who found the car are of the opinion that it was relatively new. Although the registration plates are not available to prove it. I think someone is being very fucking devious. They didn't want that car to be found.'

'I don't think they're being devious. I think they want to keep us faffing about trying to discover who our victim is for as long as possible.'

'It looks like they're succeeding. Take the next right. It's a small bog road and it's a bit ropey. Keep your speed low.'

The road she turned onto shouldn't be called a road. It was a single track allowing a car or tractor to access the bog.

'I hope you brought your wellingtons,' Glennan said. 'There's a bit of a tramp from the end of the road to the location of the car.'

'Now you tell me. And stop calling this track a road.'

'A hundred yards ahead there's a small widening in the track that will allow you to turn.'

The bog had been cut to two feet below the ground level and ricks of turf were already stacked at intervals. The foetid smell of vegetal decomposition hit Fiona with a wave of nostalgia. As a small child, she'd been sent each year for a two-week holiday to her aunt and uncle who owned a small farm in a remote area. She remembered the weather was always fine and every day she went with her uncle to help stack the sods of turf. She hadn't been allowed near the special two-sided spade known as a sleán which was used to cut the sods. When they returned to the farmhouse, on the table there would be a creel of new potatoes smothered in freshly churned butter. Her aunt and uncle were dead now. They left the farm to the prodigal son who was living in England. He had no interest in the farm and sold it off. She hadn't been there since they died. Maybe it was time for a nostalgic visit. That was the trouble with Connemara. Every sight and sound brought back memories of her childhood and contributed to her love-hate relationship with the area.

She stopped at the point suggested by Glennan and looked around the bog. 'Where's the car?'

Glennan pointed at a small hillock ahead. 'About a half-mile in that direction.'

Fiona sighed.

'What's wrong with you? It's a fine day for a walk across a bog.'

Fiona looked down at her new trainers. Seventy-five quids worth.

They exited the car and started to walk across the bog. Fiona tried to stick to the heathery scraw and avoid the dark-brown pools of water that littered their path. Inevitably, she stepped into a few and got wet to her ankles. Finally, they reached the hillock and saw the scorched car nestling in a water-laden bog hole.

'How the hell did they get the car to here?' Fiona couldn't make out the badge on the front it was badly melted.

'They drove it until it collapsed. This section of the bog hasn't been worked. Maybe the owner has passed away. Whoever dumped the car chose well. If the lad working on the bog hadn't seen smoke rising, we might never have found it.'

'Without the plates, what chance do we have of identifying it?'

As she approached the car, the smell of burned plastic and rubber got stronger.

'It has the shape of a Volkswagen,' Glennan said. 'It would have been a nice little motor if someone hadn't set it alight. Maybe the engine number is readable. Whoever did this had a bit of practice. It's too good a job for a first-timer. Maybe we're jumping to conclusions thinking it's connected to the murdered man.'

Fiona stood on the edge of the bog hole and examined the wreck. 'That would make it one hell of a coincidence and like I keep saying I don't believe in coincidences. The technical bureau guys won't like this location.'

Glennan looked around. 'You think they're going to find a cigarette butt with someone's DNA on it. Forget it. I'll call one of the locals who has a tractor and get him to pull it out to the road where they can give it the once over without getting their feet wet. My guess is that the conflagration destroyed any bit of evidence that might have been in it. If we manage to get the engine number, we'll say a prayer that the victim didn't purchase the car last week and hasn't got around to re-registering it.'

'We don't need to think up problems before we encounter them. Call your local friend and get it pulled out to dry ground.' She turned around and her foot went straight into a bog hole.

Glennan made a bad attempt at suppressing a smile. 'Next time remember the wellingtons.'

THE LOCAL MAN with the tractor arrived half an hour later and he set to work at hauling the car out of the deep bog then over the hillock before depositing it on a dry area of grass ten metres from Fiona's car. It was apparent that the operative had done this before. No money changed hands and the tractor driver left as soon as his job was complete.

'I suppose there'll be a quid pro quo somewhere down the line,' Fiona said as she watched the tractor depart.

'I suppose so.' Glennan moved to the car and examined the interior.

'A very professional job. I doubt our friends from the technical bureau will find anything worth reporting.' He went to the rear and prised the boot open, reached his hand inside, withdrew a blackened mass, and tossed it on the grass.

'What is it?'

'I think it might have been a small suitcase but given its state, I'm not certain. There's a smell of accelerant in the boot which means whoever torched the car knew the bag was there and he wanted to destroy it.'

'What the hell is going on here?'

'Someone is trying to give you a massive headache.'

'Well, they're succeeding. Where the hell are the forensic team? They should be here by now.' Fiona's stomach was telling her it was lunchtime.

Glennan took out his mobile. 'I'll get the station to check.'

Fiona examined the blackened mass that Glennan had dumped on the ground. It had fused together and it was difficult to assess what it might have been. It was too small to be a suitcase but an overnight bag was a distinct possibility. Was there a chance that there was some item remaining that would identify the victim? She doubted it but it was grasp-at-straws time.

Glennan cut the call. 'They missed the turn and went further on. They're on the way back and one of my lads is parked at the turn.'

'Time I was heading back to Galway.'

'I'll hang on here. You'd best get a move on. The forensics are in a van and there won't be room for you to pass on the bog road.'

'I'll be in touch.' Fiona slid into the driver's seat. 'Tell your lad to keep them on the road until I get through.'

Glennan saluted.

CHAPTER TWENTY-ONE

Fiona waved at the technical van as she turned onto the main road and headed back towards Clifden. She was convinced that the burned-out car and the murder victim were connected. Although the forensic team might find something that would help her identify the victim, the cursory examination that she and Glennan had made indicated that the person or persons that had torched the car had been efficient. Her only hope was that the engine number would be readable and they might be able to trace the owner. She was afraid that it might be a forlorn hope. As she approached the Connors' camp, she pulled off the road and parked behind the last caravan in the line. The camp was quiet and she noted the absence of children and cars. She exited her car, went to Maggie Connors' caravan and knocked on the door.

'Oh, it's you.' Maggie stood in the doorway.

'Who were you expecting?'

'I thought that arsehole of a sergeant might have dropped the complaint against Phil.'

'He'll get off when he appears before the judge.'

'And in the meantime.'

'You can enjoy a little holiday in beautiful Connemara.'

'We should be on our way. Our passage back to England has been booked.'

'That can be changed. Where is everybody?'

'In church, the priest is giving a blessing before we head off. It's a traveller tradition.'

'And you're an atheist?'

'What do you want this time? Another crime wave hit the area?'

'I'm not here on an official visit, I came to let you know that the local guards have solved the crime wave and found the culprits for the break-ins, two local teenagers.'

'It wasn't the travellers after all. That must have been a surprise to the locals. Maybe we're not such bad people.'

'Nobody said you were bad people.'

'But we have a reputation.'

'We all have reputations and mud sticks.'

Maggie looked at Fiona's car. 'Where's that handsome partner of yours?'

'He's back in Galway. You've heard about the murder at the horse fair.'

'I've heard about nothing else.' She laughed. 'Maybe someone insulted another man's pony. People take their animals seriously. But I suppose one shouldn't joke about a subject as serious as murder.'

'You heard it was murder.'

'That's what they're saying. I've got the kettle on, would you like a cup of tea?' She moved back into the caravan without waiting for a reply.

'Thanks.' Fiona pulled the door shut behind her. What have you heard?'

'The usual gossip. Man gets murdered and the travellers are in the area. It must be them who killed him.'

Fiona took a picture of the dead man from her pocket. 'Do you recognise him?'

Maggie took the photo and examined it carefully.

Fiona thought she saw a hint of sadness in Maggie's eyes.

She handed back the photo. 'There's something familiar. But I don't think so. Take a seat.' She poured water from the kettle into a teapot and set it on the table before adding two mugs, a sugar bowl and a bottle of milk. She sat facing Fiona. 'You think a traveller did it. That's why you're here.'

'I don't know who did it but I'm going to find them whoever it is. Someone burned out a car in the bog not far from here. I came to examine it before the forensic boys got their hands on it.' She examined Maggie's face. Her expression never changed.

Maggie poured the tea and added milk and sugar to her mug. 'Must be tough for you being a copper.'

'How so?'

'You being gay among all the testosterone boys.'

Fiona sipped her tea. 'What makes you think I'm gay?'

'Your partner is a good-looking boy and yet there isn't an ounce of sexual tension between you. To quote old Peggy, you don't have the look of love between you. You're either a cold fish or men aren't your thing. I bet you're open about it.'

'You're more like Peggy than you think. Maybe marrying a traveller has given you the gift of second sight.'

Maggie laughed. 'I don't think so.'

'I think you got to my good-looking partner for a while. I don't know you, but my guess is that you're good at attracting men.'

'I'm an old married woman for God's sake.'

'But you exude a certain sexuality.'

'Are you coming on to me?'

Fiona laughed. 'You're not my type.'

'What is your type?'

'That would be telling. Were you at the horse fair?'

'I went into town for a few hours. You've seen one horse fair you've seen them all.'

'All your vehicles have UK registrations. Is that where you're usually based?'

'Yes.'

'Where exactly?'

It's a little place called Screveton in the back of beyond in Nottinghamshire. That's spelt S-C-R-E-V-E-T-O-N when you're writing it in your little book.

'And the row between Ted Furey and your husband?'

'Drink, something in the past, I don't think they even know themselves.'

'Then why come to the same fair?'

'Why not?' She finished her tea and stood. 'We should do this again some time.'

Fiona finished her tea. 'We definitely will.'

Maggie collected the mugs and dropped them in the sink. 'Peggy said you were surrounded by death. I'm beginning to think she was right. You have a way with you that might put people on their guard.'

'Thanks for the tea and the chat. Apologies for the other day.'

'Will you be letting the Fureys know they're innocent of the break-ins?'

'I will indeed.'

CHAPTER TWENTY-TWO

Fiona arrived back at the station at half past two. She picked up a smoked salmon sandwich and a coffee on the way and started into her lunch as soon as she sat at her desk.

'What's the story?' Tracy said.

'The car is a total wipe-out. Whoever burned it out drove it into a bog and we had the Devil's own job in pulling it out.' She washed a mouthful of sandwich down with a slug of coffee before lifting her leg and showing off her ruined trainers. 'The arsehole drove it into an uncut area that was littered with bog holes. These trainers cost me seventy-five quid.'

'They'll dry out.'

'You really think so? Shows what you know about the reaction between new trainers and stale bog water.'

'But the car is connected to our murder victim?'

'I assume so, otherwise it's a hell of a coincidence if a relatively new car is burned out the same day we discover a dead body.'

'Maybe there's still some evidence in the car.'

'It's a possibility. The technicians are on site but it looked like there wasn't much to find.'

'Another dead end.'

'Another?'

'I've been through the TV footage. There's only one sight of the murdered man.' He showed her the still he had printed off.

'He's on his own.'

'That's the way it looks. He could be looking at someone across the road.'

'He could indeed.' She stared at the photo while taking the last bite from her sandwich and draining her coffee. She tossed the detritus into the wastepaper basket. 'So far, we're in the shit.' She was getting the feeling that the case would end up in the unsolved file. Please, God, she prayed, give us something to work with.

'There's a photographer in Oughterard that specialises in photographing horse fairs. He has a load on his website. I tried to get in contact but he's out on a shoot. I left a message on his voicemail.'

'What about Instagram and Facebook?'

'I'm going to start looking there.'

Fiona noticed the lack of enthusiasm. 'Someone out there knows who our victim is. Let's get the sketch artist in and have a likeness made from the photos. I need to talk to Horgan about putting it out on TV. I'd better brief him on the car.'

'SHITE.' Horgan slammed his palm against his desk. 'We can't catch a break on this one.'

'We're not supposed to catch a break.' Fiona was sitting across from him. 'Whoever murdered him wanted us to lose time finding out who he is. They know that the longer we run around like chickens with our heads chopped off the better chance they have of getting away scot-free. I received the preliminary forensics from the site. They collected two bin bags of rubbish, mainly used drink and food containers. They're sifting through it but don't get your hopes up. He was wearing an expensive jacket but the labels had been cut out, and his shirt, pullover and shoes could be bought in any shop.'

'That doesn't give us much to work with.'

'It doesn't give us anything to work with. I'm getting a bad feeling with this one. The clean-up is a little *too* professional. In other words, I don't think this is a run-of-the-mill murder.'

'What sort of murder is run-of-the-mill in your mind?'

'Husband, wife, friend, colleague, the kind of thing we're used to. It might be drugs but it's definitely something criminal. The lack of identification on the body, the burning of the car. They knew what they were doing. They even emptied his pockets. He bought a burger and a beer. He'd probably have had change but they cleaned him out.'

'Might have been robbery?'

Fiona was lost in thought. 'Why did the killer empty his pockets?'

Horgan cleared his throat. 'I said it might have been a robbery.'

'Sorry, boss, yes it might have been a robbery. It very probably was. But what did he have on him that was worth stealing.' There was a thought trying to break through the fog in Fiona's mind. She tried to grab it but it kept flitting away. 'Tracy's been through two hours of video footage from the horse fair and there's only one sighting of the victim. We're hoping to collect photos from both professional and amateur photographers and that's our next line of enquiry.' She showed Horgan the print Tracy had made. 'He's looking at something across the road but it could have been anything.'

'It doesn't look good. What do I tell the Park?'

'We're following a definite line of enquiry.'

'That would be a lie.'

Fiona stood. 'I know.'

CHAPTER TWENTY-THREE

Fiona was sitting at the table looking at the remains of a roasted chicken when she felt Aisling's hands massaging the two sides of her neck.

'Your neck muscles are so tight. Relax and I'll loosen them.'

'I didn't know that you practised massage.'

'I don't but if I start asking questions, you'll accuse me of playing the clinical psychologist. And that's not part of our relationship.'

'That's the problem with our relationship, you'll never stop being the clinical psychologist and I'll never stop being the cop.'

'What has you so stressed?'

'He's going to get away with murder.'

'Who's going to get away with murder?' Aisling continued to knead Fiona's neck muscles.

'God, but that feels good. The bastard who killed the unknown man in Clifden. We've been on the case two days and we still can't put a name to the murdered man. He has no identification on him, his pockets were empty and we think that his car was burned out on a bog. Our whole police procedure is founded on having the identity of the victim so we can develop the motive, means and opportunity that are the cornerstones of the method. I know I'm a good detective but whoever murdered that man is trying to ensure that I never get this case off the ground. I'm damned if I'll let him succeed.'

'Someone knows who the victim is. You just have to find that someone.'

'I'm trying.' Fiona moved her head forward and disengaged Aisling's hands. 'Thanks for the rub.'

'Have you been to the dojo?'

'Not in the past few days.'

'Go tomorrow morning. The exercise will help and if your mind is at rest, you might come up with the answer to your problem.'

'Maybe you're right.' She stood up, turned to face Aisling and hugged her. 'What would I do without you?'

'I won't go to Dublin this weekend.'

'Yes, you will. You need to reconcile with your family.'

'Maybe I'm fooling myself. Things will never go back to what they were. I'll always be the daughter who left her family to set up house with her lesbian lover.'

'Life moves on and so do relationships. Nothing remains the same and the relationship that you forge now might be a more honest and long-lasting one.'

'I never had you pegged as a philosopher. I'm aware that life moves on. My ex walked out of divorce court and into the church across the road to get married. That's not quite true. I think he waited a week. It was a sign of his great love for me that he waited so long. Those who move on quickest are the ones that already have a new life planned.' She sat down heavily at the table. 'I spend most of my days asking people what they think they should do to solve their problems. I suppose I should spend some time taking my own advice. I miss my parents. I used to think that their views were associated with an Ireland that no longer exists. But I see the looks we get when we walk hand-in-hand down Shop Street. They're not bigots by choice. They haven't read about sexuality. They've taken the Church's view and made it their own.'

'By inviting you to their party, they've sent a signal and opened a door. I would have like to have been invited but maybe they're not ready for that yet. But you're going and you'll make the most of the opportunity.'

'We're quite a pair. Your mother lives a few miles down the road and you won't visit her. Some days I look at the photos of my parents and think that the time is running out. Do you ever do that?'

'I have no photos to look at. She gave away my son. I can never forgive her for that.'

'But she stayed with you. Your mother did what she was told. I'll go to Dublin if you go to see your mother.'

'I'll think about it. Let's clean up and find some mindless piece of crap on TV. Tomorrow is another day and maybe your prescription of a few hours in the dojo will bear fruit. Even if I doubt it.'

CHAPTER TWENTY-FOUR

When the doors of the dojo opened at seven o'clock, Fiona was the first person through. She spent the first hour working herself through katas and practising with one of the judo instructors. For the second hour, she acted as an assistant to the sensei teaching a class of teenagers then took a quick shower and rode over to Mill Street. She felt energised but the logjam in her mind concerning the case hadn't moved one inch. She picked up two coffees and Danishes and her step was light as she made her way to the squad room.

'Thanks.' Tracy took a coffee and a pastry. 'You've been working out.' He looked her up and down. 'You look good.'

'Less of that, haven't you been reading the graffiti on the men's toilets lately. Don't tell me I'm no longer featuring.'

'You're still flavour-of-the-month and if I ever find out who the shithouse poet is, I guarantee he won't be able to put Sharpie to wall for quite a long time.'

'Let's not spoil the fun of some mindless bugger. A good thrashing won't make him a better person.'

Tracy took a bite of his Danish and sipped his coffee. 'The tox screen came in this morning. The only point of note is that there was a trace of benzodiazepine in his urine.'

'What the hell is that?'

'Did you ever hear of temazepam?'

'No.'

'My uncle is scared shitless of flying. As soon as he's belted up in his seat, he drops a temazepam and he's out like a light. He wakes up in Crete and mises the whole flight experience. I looked it up and temazepam is a benzodiazepine. It slows the brain down. It's sometimes diagnosed for insomnia.'

'Our victim was drugged.'

'Or he had trouble sleeping.'

'Funny boy. I was wondering how someone got close enough to stick a knife into him. He's a burly lad and he would have put up a decent fight. So we know a few facts about our assailant. He felt he needed an edge in order to take the victim down and he knew how to handle a knife. According to the pathologist, the placing of the wound was nearly perfect. It might not have been his first murder. Let's get it up on the whiteboard.'

Tracy added the information to the few facts already on the board.

Fiona stood beside him. Tracy had added the photos taken where the body had been dumped and the fingerprints as well as the results of the post-mortem.

'I stopped by Maggie Connors on my way back from the bog yesterday.' Fiona said. 'I showed her a photo of our victim. I might be wrong but I saw a hint of recognition in her eyes before she closed it down. I think she knew I'd seen it because she spent a good while looking at the photo and then said she might have seen him somewhere. She didn't want to give me a definite no.'

'You keep coming back to her. You got a bee in your bonnet there.'

'Graduate of Trinity College runs off with a traveller. That doesn't happen every day.'

'What about the custom in traditional music of the lord's lady running away with a gypsy?'

'That was my line. Did you ever notice that it doesn't end happily? The lord eventually finds them and kills them both.'

'Maybe she loves that brute with the scar on his face. Don't you believe in love?'

'I think Maggie believes in love. She had you eating out of her hand as soon as you met her.'

Tracy turned his face away. 'That's not true.'

'Dressed in a dirty old Trinity hoodie with her feet planted in a pair of wellies, she captured your attention. Can you imagine the effect she'd have if she was all scrubbed up and dressed to the nines? Women like Maggie exude sex. She'll probably still be attracting young men when she a grey-haired old lady.'

'That is if you don't put her in prison for murder.'

'If I can prove that she murdered our victim, I'd do it in a heartbeat.'

'You do think that she's involved.'

'I didn't say that. I think she may have recognised our victim. And that raises all kinds of intriguing possibilities. I don't think that Phil Connors would take kindly to another man chasing his wife.'

Her phone rang and she grabbed the handset. 'Madden.' She picked up a pen and started to write. 'Thanks, anything else.' She replaced the handset in the cradle. 'Our colleagues in the technical bureau managed to get an engine number from the car.' She handed Tracy the paper she'd written on. The car was a Volkswagen Golf, the tech thinks it might be six or seven years old. Get on the phone to the local Volkswagen dealer and find out what he can tell us.

'What are you going to do?'

'I'm going to think about how Maggie Connors figures in this thing.'

CHAPTER TWENTY-FIVE

They had passed the magic forty-eight hours and Fiona knew that a break was necessary to preserve any momentum that they had already established. If Maggie Connors had recognised the victim, there was a fifty per cent chance she might have met him during her time working for the National Travellers Service. She knew she was suffering from myopia. For all she knew, the murdered man could be a butcher from Athlone who was murdered by his brother-in-law at the behest of his sister. Until she had more information, any scenario however wild or improbable was possible. But Maggie Connors had given herself an escape route by saying that she might have met the dead man. Fiona was too experienced to expect evidence to fall into her lap. But she was beginning to panic. She took the file and started from the first page. An hour later, she closed the file without having had a moment of enlightenment.

Tracy dropped a sheet of paper on her desk. 'The local Volkswagen dealer put me onto the main office in Wolfsburg. I haven't a word of German but luckily one of the sales staff spoke good English. The car was exported to England. He traced it to the dealer who gave me the registration and the registration document that he called the V5C.' He pointed to two numbers on the page. 'I went on one of those car-check sites. That's what I got from them.' Tracy put a sheet he had printed off in front of Fiona. There were two columns of text. The first column contained five items: the date when the former owner sold the car, the date when the former keeper bought the car, the number of former keepers as per the logbook, the city where the vehicle was registered by the Driver and Vehicle Licencing Agency in Swansea and the vehicle's age. Fiona examined the information in the second column. There was no information on the current owner.

'I checked with Revenue to see if the car had been imported into Ireland. It wasn't. It's still registered in the United Kingdom.'

Fiona looked at the page again. 'In Nottingham.' She was lost in thought for a few moments. 'Bring up a map of England on the computer.'

Tracy hit a few keys and a map of England appeared on the screen. What was the name of that place that Maggie Connors told you they're normally based.'

'Screveton.' She spelt it out for him. 'Find it.'

Tracy did a search and a red arrow appeared on the screen. He zoomed in on the area surrounding the arrow. 'The largest big town in the area is Nottingham.'

'Now there's a coincidence.'

Tracy sighed.

'Afraid we're going to nail Maggie for the murder?'

'For the moment it's just a coincidence.' He put up his hands in the air. 'I know, you don't like coincidences.'

'Let's make some wild assumptions. The dead man also lives in Screveton and he's well known to the Connors. He drives his car to Ireland and makes his way to Clifden where the horse fair is in full swing. He's a good-looking fellow and he didn't come to Clifden just to appreciate the horse flesh. Let's say he's here to pursue a tryst with the beautiful Maggie and Phil gets wind of it. Phil doesn't look like the kind of guy that would take kindly to someone meddling with his wife. He had family members about. They lift our victim, work him over and kill him. They remove everything that will identify him and dump the body. They assume, correctly, that we'll have a hell of a job identifying an anonymous body that has no local ties. They even empty his pockets in case we find some English coins or notes. They drive the car deep into the bog and torch it. It fits.'

'It's plausible. But we have no evidence to support any of it.'

'Then we better go about getting the evidence. Is there a cop shop in Screveton?'

'I have no idea.'

'Then find out.'

Tracy turned back to the computer. 'Doesn't look like it. The area is mainly farmland. Doesn't look like there's much in Screveton itself.'

'Get onto Nottinghamshire Police and see if they're ready to give us a hand at identifying our victim.'

'What are you going to do?'

'I'm going to make sure that neither the Connors nor the Fureys are permitted to leave the area until our enquiries are complete.'

'Does that mean you're going to be outside the office again on your own?'

'Are you afraid that I'll get lost? I made a mistake yesterday. Maggie asked me whether I would give the Fureys the same message about the two boys who were arrested for the local burglaries. I said I would and I didn't. That was a mistake I intend to rectify.'

CHAPTER TWENTY-SIX

Another day, another trip into Connemara, Fiona thought as she drove out of Galway. Maybe it was the early morning session in the dojo or maybe it was the fact that she felt they might be getting somewhere on the investigation but she felt lighter mentally and she sped through Moycullen, Oughterard and on to Clifden. Tracy was right of course. They didn't have a shred of evidence to back up the scenario she had laid out. But it was a start.

'It's plausible.' Glennan handed Fiona a saucer with a cup of tea on it and a ginger nut biscuit on the side.

'The question is, can we keep the Connors and Fureys in town until we can put some flesh on the bones.'

'I suppose we could prolong the arrest of Phil Connors and Ted Furey but that won't make me popular with the townspeople. In order to keep them indefinitely, I'll need to upgrade the complaint to one of aggravated assault and when it goes before the judge, I might get a royal kick up the arse for manufacturing a storm in a teacup. And then there's the chief super to consider and if the assistant commissioner hears about it, I'll be forced to explain that you cajoled me into it as you were close to nailing the culprit. You are close to nailing the culprit?'

'We're certainly closer.' She dunked half her biscuit in her tea and ate it. 'If we manage to identify our victim, and if he turns out to be a traveller known to both the Connors and the Fureys, then we'll be on our way.'

'That's a hell of a lot of ifs. I think there needs to be a lot of work done on linking the dead man to the Connors or the Fureys. They have a lot of experience of dealing with the police and they're not about to roll over. Neither will they implicate each other. There's already a feud between the two families and one snitching on the other could lead to an all-out war.'

'So are we agreed?'

Glennan sipped his tea. 'As soon as you leave this office, I'm going to check my pension situation. I'm an amateur potter and I'm always swearing to take it up properly. Problem is I have a wife and two kids at college. You might just be forcing an issue here.'

'From our limited experience of each other, I think that might be a loss for the Garda. You'll do the necessary?'

Glennan put his teacup on his desk and made the sign of the cross. 'Stupid man that I am, I will.'

Fiona finished her tea and stood. 'You're a sound man. When this is over, you'll have to show me some of your work. I'm in the market for a new set of coffee cups.'

'Please leave, I have to write a fiction that the judge might not throw back in my face.'

FIONA WAS BACK in her car and driving on through the town. The annual influx of visitors was in full swing and the town's commercial sector had come to life. The shops that had been shut for the winter had had their cobwebs removed and now presented their best face to the visitors. Fiona knew that the locals welcomed the invasion of foreign visitors and staycationers from other parts of Ireland but they also resented having their sleepy town taken over by holidaymakers. She was also aware that the town's leading citizens would be banging on Glennan's door to protest about his decision to restrict the movements of the travellers. She passed through the centre and made her way along the coast to where the Furey clan was camped. As she parked in a gap between two caravans, it was clear that the county council would have a job on their hands returning the site to pristine countryside. She exited her car and found herself surrounded by a coterie of Furey children. Some of the elder ones were openly aggressive, asking her what she was doing in their camp. The younger ones looked out at her from behind their elder brothers and sisters. She pushed her way through the mob and entered the open area behind the caravans where she had last seen the head of the clan at his card game. The children stood around her in a circle but there wasn't an adult in sight. After a couple of minutes, a caravan door opened and the rotund figure of Ted Furey stepped out of a modern mobile home.

'Leave the poor woman alone,' Furey shouted as he walked in her direction. 'Go off and play somewhere else.'

The children muttered but obeyed their features downcast. Fiona smiled as they departed. She had no time for brats. She liked children at a remove. The planet was going down the plughole at an increasing rate and what sensible person wanted to bring a child into a world that was choking itself to death. Even in her teens, she'd despaired at the direction the world was taking. The fact that she had borne a child had nothing to do with her desire to repopulate the planet. She had been compelled through a combination of rape and religion to bring a child into the world against her will.

'What brings you back?' Furey said.

No tea and cake on offer here, Fiona thought. 'I wanted to give you an apology on behalf of the Garda Síochána.'

'I suppose there's a first time for everything. What did you do wrong?'

'The Garda arrested two local teenagers for the spate of burglaries in the area. There was a feeling that your clan or the Connors were responsible and we mistakenly went along with that assumption.'

'That's big of you. Who twisted your arm? Are the locals afraid that we might take umbrage? You've had your say, you'd best be on your way.'

'Now that I'm here, I suppose you heard we found a dead body on the side of the main road.'

'It's the talk of the town.'

She took a photo of the dead man's face from her pocket and handed it to him. 'We haven't been able to identify the man yet. You don't recognise him by any chance?'

Furey took the photo, looked at it and handed it back. 'Never saw the bloke in my life.'

Fiona took the photo and looked around at the cars and the caravans all of which bore English registration plates. 'You normally live in England.'

'We come for the horse fair and to meet other travellers.'

'But all your cars and caravans are registered in England so you must live there.'

'I suppose we do.'

'Where?'

'None of your business.'

'I don't think either of us want to go down the road of making it my business.'

'All over. We don't have a particular site.'

'You ever stay in Screveton?'

'There's a big traveller site there. We've been there.'

Fiona put the photo away. Furey hadn't shown any reaction to it.

'Are you the reason we're being kept here?'

'No, I have no business with you. I heard you had a fight with Phil Connors and you're both up before the judge.'

'Fight my arse. We never laid hands on each other.'

'Tell it to the judge. I'm sure he'll be impressed and maybe let you off with a fine. What's the reason for the conflict between you?'

'I don't rightly know but we don't like seeing each other around. Phil Connors is a bit of a coward. Boxer has called him out dozens of times but Connors won't fight.'

'A bit stupid isn't it. Both of you are continuing a feud and neither of you knows what the initial argument was about.'

'It's our way. Settled people like you don't understand the tradition. We live and die by our traveller ways.'

'Thanks for your time.' Fiona extended her hand.

Furey turned his back. 'You'd best be off before the children come back.'

CHAPTER TWENTY-SEVEN

On the way back to Galway, Fiona replayed her interview with Ted Furey. He hadn't given any sign of recognition when he'd examined the photo. Was there really any reason to suspect that he knew the dead man? The burned-out car had been registered in Nottingham but did that mean that the owner lived in Screveton? Was she making a mountain out of a molehill? She was so desperate for a lead she was grasping at the first straw that blew past her in the wind. There was also the fact that she might be suffering from a case of ethnic profiling. There was no reason why she should be continually trying to put the Connors and the Fureys in the frame for the murder. The way she'd colluded with Glennan to hold the travellers in the area was pushing her obsession to the limit. It was just as likely that some resident of Clifden was responsible for the murder. In which case, he, or she, might be thousands of miles away by now. The dopamine had been flowing since Tracy discovered the registration for the burned-out car. She was feeling the onset of a crash. Perhaps she had been deluding herself.

Her mobile rang and she saw Tracy's number on the

screen. She pulled into the side of the road and put on her hazard lights. 'What?'

'Where are you?'

'Halfway back to the station. What's up?'

'I've been on to Nottinghamshire Police. The desk sergeant the operator put me onto wasn't impressed by my rank. Either that or Brexit has kicked in hard. I told him our problem and offered to send a photo of the dead man and a set of his fingerprints on the wire. He gave me one of those info at Nottinghamshire Police email addresses. The kind that nobody bothers their arse to read, or answer.'

'Another dead end. Have you heard anything back from the National Crime Agency?'

'Not a peep. Maybe our victim isn't in their database.'

'Maybe I assumed too much. It was worth a try.'

'We're running out of avenues to explore.'

'Don't I know it.'

'The final autopsy report came in.'

'I'll look at it when I get back.'

'Anything on your end?'

'No. I'll grab some lunch on the way back. See you early afternoon.' She ended the call and re-joined the road. She hadn't yet reached the cut-off for Glenmore and some force other than her own mind made her take the right-hand turn and travel the fifteen kilometres to her native village. She convinced herself that it had been the thought of a ham and cheese sandwich and a pot of tea, and the use of the toilet at Tigh Jimmy that had made her take the Glenmore option.

Jimmy looked up from cleaning the bar as she entered. The two men who habitually occupied the end of the bar stopped speaking and watched her as she walked past.

'A ham and cheese sandwich and a pot of tea.' She marched towards the rear of the lounge. 'Is the bog clean?'

'Just mopped it out myself.'

When she re-entered the bar, she sat at a table in the middle of the lounge, aware of the stares of the customers.

Jimmy deposited a pot of tea, a cup and saucer, a milk jug and a sugar bowl on the table and sat facing her.

'I suppose that I'm persona non grata in Glenmore.' She poured tea into the cup.

'If that means what I think it does, I don't think that the locals are taking up a collection to erect a statue in your honour at the crossroads.'

'I did my job. The Folans got what they deserved.'

'What brings you here?'

'I was on the way to Galway and I had the need of the toilet.'

'There are plenty of toilets in Oughterard and Moycullen.'

'I heard that you make a decent ham and cheese sandwich.'

Jimmy stood and walked to the bar, returned two minutes later and set a plate with a thick-cut sandwich in front of her. He retook his seat. 'When are you going to get a bit of sense?'

'What do you mean?'

'She's getting old.'

'We're all ageing at the same pace.'

'There's a rumour around the village. They say that she's received a letter from your father. He's sick and he wants to come home. Why does every emigrant want to die in this country? Can't they just die in the place they spent most of their lives? The ones that don't want to die here want to be buried here or have the ashes scattered over the old sod.'

'I hope she told him to piss off.'

'No daughterly love there.'

'He left us to fend for ourselves. Now he wants to come back and be nursed in his last days. What about the doxy he lived with beyond?'

'Probably doesn't want the job of cleaning up after him. I think it's time that you had a word with your mother.'

'Maybe I will.'

Jimmy stood. 'Good girl. The tea is on the house and the sandwich is a fiver.'

She took out her purse and paid. She looked at the sandwich and realised that the news about her father's return had caused her to lose her appetite. 'Pack up the sandwich for me, my eyes were bigger than my stomach.'

Jimmy took the plate and returned to the bar.

The fact that her estranged father wanted to return had hit her with the force of a sledgehammer. She had excised him from her life and had no desire to ever meet him again. He had ceased to exist for her. She was a product of his seed and that was the end of it. But was that enough to get her to reconcile with her mother? She finished her tea, stood and collected her sandwich at the bar.

'Don't be a stranger,' Jimmy said as he handed over a bag containing her lunch.

CHAPTER TWENTY-EIGHT

Fiona dropped the bag containing the sandwich on Tracy's desk. 'It's one of Jimmy's specials.'

'Thanks, I already had lunch but I'll save it for later.'

She looked over his shoulder at the computer screen which was full of small icons depicting photographs. 'What are you up to?'

'We received a couple of responses to our request for photos taken at the horse fair. I've been viewing them.'

'Any sign of the victim?'

Tracy shook his head.

She sat at her desk. There was an A4 manila envelope with her name on the front on her keyboard. She picked it up and opened it. The contents consisted of three typed pages, more than a dozen photos of the body and a series of X-rays. She read the typed papers which didn't add to what she already knew. The bruises on the torso were antemortem and were received three to five days before death. She flipped quickly through the photos which they had already received by email. The last two pages consisted of the X-rays taken by the pathologist's assistant. There were two pages with four X-rays on each page. She laid them out on her desk. The pictures were not original but reduced and printed on an A4 sheet. She had no medical knowledge so examining the X-rays was the equivalent of looking into a bush. She was about to add the report to the file when she saw a mark on one of the X-rays. She turned to Tracy. 'Give me that magnifying glass.'

He tossed it over and she caught it.

She concentrated on the dead man's left arm. There was a dark mark on it. 'What the hell is that?'

'What are you looking at?' Tracy asked.

'Damned if I know but it looks like there's something on the bone of his left arm.'

Fiona opened her desk drawer and took out Professor Daly's card. She dialled the number and the phone was answered by a secretary. 'I need to speak to Professor Daly urgently.'

'She's giving a lecture.'

'When will she be finished?'

'In ten minutes give or take. It depends on the number of questions she takes.'

'Tell her to call me immediately.' She gave her direct number. 'I mean immediately.'

'I get the message.'

Fiona replaced the handset. If what she was looking at was a metal plate, she knew that it would have a code embossed on it that indicated the location of the operation and a patient number. She picked up the magnifying glass again and brought the arm into the highest focus but the picture was too small to clearly verify her assumption. She snatched up the phone when it rang. 'Professor Daly?'

'Yes, my secretary said it was urgent.'

'I've read your autopsy report and examined the X-rays you took of our murder victim. There are several pictures per page and I've had to use a magnifying glass. I may be wrong but I think I see a steel plate in the picture showing his left arm.'

'I'm sorry but I haven't had time to examine the X-rays myself. Give me a few seconds to bring them up on my computer.'

Fiona waited nervously while she listened to computer keys being pressed.

'Oh God, you're right. There is a metal plate in his left arm. It looks like he had a compound fracture at some point. I'm terribly sorry that this slipped through. My assistant should have flagged that.'

'Am I right in thinking that the plate will have a code on it that will identify the hospital where the procedure was carried out and an identifier for the patient?'

'Yes, that should be the case.'

'Can you read the code from the picture on the computer?'

'I've zoomed in and the marks on the plate are clear.' She read off a series of numbers.

'How do we decipher these?'

'It's not my field. I'll have to consult with a colleague.'

'Will you do it straight away? It could identify our victim.'

'I'll call the orthopaedic consultant.'

The line went dead. This could be the break they were hoping for. The murderer had been so damn clever removing all the identification but there was no way he could have known about the metal plate. Fiona waited impatiently for the phone to ring. She watched the minute hand on the office clock click forward. Finally, the phone rang and she snatched it from the cradle.

'You're in luck. The procedure was performed here at University Hospital. My colleague is locating the name of the patient. He'll text me when he has it. You really should obtain this information by issuing a warrant. But I accept that I was culpable this time. I'd appreciate it if you didn't broadcast that you got the information through the back door. The text has just arrived; the man's name is Dermot Ward, date of birth twentieth October 1991. No address. That's it. Goodbye.'

'What did that guy in the bath shouted when he discovered something?' Fiona said.

'Eureka,' Tracy said. 'Why?'

Fiona marched to the whiteboard, took a black marker and wrote "Dermot Ward, DOB 20/10/1991". 'That's our victim and I want to know everything about him in the next twenty-four hours. He had his arm fixed in Galway. So let's start with the Department of Social Welfare and Revenue. He might have worked and paid taxes.'

'I don't want to burst your balloon but Ward is a traveller name and that means that he might not be registered with either Social Welfare or Revenue.'

'That could be another coincidence that's not really a coincidence. Maybe it's just another piece of the puzzle. Whatever it is, I want you on the computer. I want to know everything about him from his birth till his death.'

'I think it's time that you spoke to Horgan about reinforcements.'

CHAPTER TWENTY-NINE

Horgan leaned back in his ergonomic chair. 'Good work,' he said, a smile as wide as Galway Bay plastered on his face. 'And he's a tinker you say.'

'Boss,' Fiona said. 'Tracy already told you not to use that word. It's what they call a pejorative. Which means that you're characterising a certain ethnic group. And I didn't say that he was a traveller. He has a surname that is associated with a traveller clan.'

'There's a better than fifty per cent chance that he's a ti... traveller. You were right to concentrate on the two bands of travellers in Clifden.'

'I made some assumptions which might be right or wrong. Either way, it's a lead that we need to follow. We require a lot more information to confirm our suspicions. That's where you come in. We need at least two more bodies. Preferably two bodies that are computer literate.'

'Two more bodies, you and Tracy are doing fine.'

'We're not. We've lost a lot of time just finding out the name of our victim. We need to delve into his life. Maybe he crossed paths with the Connors or the Fureys. Maybe there's a feud between his clan and one of theirs. There are lots of possibilities and we'll have to look at all of them. For that we need reinforcements.'

'What about one body?'

'Two bodies minimum and over time perhaps another.'

'Is this an attempt at empire build? Do you see this increase of officers under your control as a stepping-stone to becoming an inspector?'

'That never crossed my mind,' Fiona lied. 'Everyone knows that I'm not interested in promotion. I'm only interested in solving this case.'

'But the fact that you managed a team of three officers won't harm you in front of a promotion panel.'

'If they don't consider solving the Sarah Joyce murder and the Galway burglaries, then they won't give a fiddler's how many people I managed.'

'You have a point.' He opened his desk drawer, removed a file and opened it. 'Let's see who we can spare.'

'This case is sensitive. It's not a question as to who you can spare. We need the two best bodies to throw at this investigation.'

'You're a right ball breaker, Madden.' He continued to examine the contents of the file. 'You can have Fitzsimons and Brogan. They're both experienced and computer literate.'

Fiona didn't know either officer well so she was at a disadvantage. 'Okay, but if it doesn't work out, I may need to make a change.'

'You'll take what you're given.'

Fiona stood. 'Then the result is on you. I need them today.'

'Okay, now piss off.'

CHAPTER THIRTY

Half an hour later the team were assembled around the whiteboard. She noted that neither of the new members looked particularly happy. It was a sign that her reputation had gone before her. She decided to ignore their gloomy faces. Peter Fitzsimons was that rarity in the Garda Síochána: a fifty-two-year-old who had spent his whole career on the bottom rung of the ladder and his whole demeanour screamed "lifer". He was overweight with a gut that should have carried a health warning and his wrinkled brown suit might have fitted him perfectly twenty years ago. His tie, which was loose around his substantial neck, was spotted with dark stains that Fiona hoped was food. His face was pale and round and tired. When he'd joined Fiona at the whiteboard, she had silently cursed her boss. Fintan Brogan was younger; Fiona guessed he was in his early forties, his suit was newer and his tie fitted neatly around his collar. Fiona realised that she was making assumptions of ability on criteria that were personally based. Fitzsimons had years of experience that he could add to the team and Brogan, despite his clean-cut image, might turn out to be a dud. Only time would tell. Fiona spent an hour running through the case from her and Tracy's arrival in Clifden to Daly's phone call.

'Is this a case of the tinkers did it?' Fitzsimons said when she had finished.

'We don't use words like tinkers these days,' Tracy said. 'We call them travellers and they're every bit as Irish as you or me.'

'I don't hold with all this political correctness shit,' Fitzsimons said. 'I prefer to call a spade a spade. They were called tinkers when I was a boy and that's what I'll continue to call them.'

Tracy was about to continue the conversation when Fiona shot him a glance.

'We know who the victim is but we know nothing about him,' Fiona said. 'He had his arm operation in Galway which means that he spent part of his life in the county. I want to know what he got up from the time he was born until he wound up dead.' She looked at Fitzsimons. 'I'll bet you've done some digging into people's backgrounds in your career. I want you to cover this whiteboard with information on our victim.'

'Cradle to death,' Fitzsimons said. 'I'm on it.'

'What do I do?' Brogan said. His voice was high-pitched and reminded Fiona of the footballer David Beckham.

'We're assuming that the burned-out vehicle belonged to the victim. We need to know when he arrived in Ireland and what brought him to Clifden. In other words, we need a timeline of his movements. If he came by car, he would have used a ferry. Call the companies and see if they have a booking for Dermot Ward. Then I want you to account for every moment of his time until he ended up dead.'

'What will you and Garda Tracy do?' Fitzsimons asked.

'That's my business. We'll meet here tomorrow morning and I want some preliminary results. Hop to it.'

Fitzsimons and Brogan slunk away towards their desks at the other side of the squad room.

'Not the happiest of campers,' Fiona said.

'Give them time,' Tracy said. 'I have a feeling they may have heard rumours about your management style.'

'And who might have spread those rumours given that you're the only person who reports directly to me?'

'I don't talk about you but there's a rumour about that you don't take prisoners.'

'And what do you think?'

'I think you don't take prisoners. By the way, you didn't answer Fitzsimons' question. What are you and I going to do?'

'I thought we'd reached a place in our partnership where you didn't have to be told what to do. What do you think you should do next?'

He sat down at his desk, turned on his computer, brought up the file of the photos he'd been examining earlier, and began to examine them.

'We are making progress. That's exactly what I would have suggested.' She picked up her phone and dialled Professor Daly's number. When the secretary answered, Fiona asked to speak to her boss.

'Yes,' Daly said.

'I'd like to have a copy of Ward's file.'

'Without going through the hassle of a warrant no doubt.'

'Obviously.'

'Not possible, it's a firing offence. We have a policy of strict adherence to the data protection laws.'

'I won't tell if you don't. You cost us twenty-four hours by not reading the X-rays.'

'Blackmail someone else.' The line went dead.

Fiona looked at Tracy and saw a smile on his lips.

'That went well.'

'When you're finished with the photos, you can prepare a request for Ward's medical file. But before all that I want you to send a message to your friend in Nottingham and ask him have they had any contact with a Dermot Ward and give them his DOB.'

'It'll take me most of the evening to do all that and I have other plans.'

'There's no overtime on this case. So you better get cracking if you don't want to disappoint Cliona.'

'How did you know? Don't bother answering.' He turned back to the computer screen.

CHAPTER THIRTY-ONE

Tracy was busy at his desk when Fiona left for the evening. Her two new colleagues had already departed. She checked the whiteboard and saw that Fitzsimons had added some details from Ward's birth certificate but little else. Rome wasn't built in a day. It had been the best day of the investigation so far. That hadn't been easy but at least they had reached square one, they knew the identity of the victim. It had taken them almost three days to reach this point and in that time the murderer might well be in Timbuktu. There was a procedure to be followed. Someone had wanted Ward dead and there was a reason for that desire, in other words, a motive. At some point, they would have to circulate the local pubs and restaurants in Clifden and see if some hawk-eyed waitress or bar manager remembered Ward drinking or eating with another person. They were at the start of a long road but at least they had a firm direction in mind. And there was no guarantee that they would succeed. Her air of despondency disappeared and when she read a text from Aisling suggesting a pre-dinner drink, she arranged to drop her bike home and for her partner to pick her up. The weather was holding up and it was a shame to waste the sunshine.

. . .

Pádraicíns is a large pub/restaurant set just above the sea outside the small village of Furbo. Its main attraction is that it has a large outdoor area that looks down on a popular beach and out across Galway Bay. They found seats on the terrace. The sun was setting but there was still a crowd of people on the beach and it sparkled off the water.

'So, you've cracked your case.' Aisling deposited a pint of Guinness and a well-filled glass of white wine on the table.

'I could arrest you for driving after drinking that.'

'We both know that I'm perfectly okay with one glass of wine.'

'I don't think the judge would accept that and that's more than one glass. And no, we haven't cracked our case. But we are in the game.'

'I told you things would work out.'

'I don't remember you telling me that.' Fiona held her pint aloft as a toast before taking a mouthful.

Aisling sipped her wine. 'So, overall it's been a good day. It's reflected in your improved humour.'

'What's that they say about the curate's egg, it's good in places. The case has suddenly taken off but I had lunch in Glenmore on the way back from Clifden and there's a rumour in the village that my father wants to return to Ireland. They say that he's extremely ill or even dying and he wants the wife he left more than twenty years ago to look after him.'

'You're joking. Your poor mother. I thought he'd found another woman in America.'

'So they say. But I don't suppose she saw the words "nursing old dying man" in the job description when she met him. Anyway, it's only a rumour. There's probably nothing to it.'

'You could have verified it by contacting your mother.'

'That would mean that I'd have to talk to her and that

would break a promise that I made to myself eighteen years ago.'

'We've been through this and you know how I feel. If there's even the slightest chance that your mother is going to agree to have him back, you've got to convince her to refuse.'

'She's a big girl, she can make her own decisions without my help.'

'My God but you're cold.'

Fiona looked out at the people on the beach. They all had problems. Some were small and day-to-day. Others were large and existential. She and Aisling were no different. Did she have forgiveness in her? Maybe it was time. The portents seemed to be pointing that way. Her return to Galway had put her and her mother in proximity. The murder case in Glenmore and now the possibility of her father's return. She turned and looked at Aisling. 'I suppose I am but I didn't start life like that.'

CHAPTER THIRTY-TWO

Tracy arrived at the station at eight o'clock. He'd worked late the previous evening but still hadn't managed to get the warrant for University Hospital prepared. He was keen on Cliona Gallagher and he didn't want to begin their relationship with a series of broken dates. He switched on his computer and brought up the warrant template. He'd taken the precaution to arrange a meeting with the chief super for nine o'clock to have the warrant signed. At five to nine, he was standing in O'Reilly's outer office with the warrant in his hand. At nine o'clock on the dot, O'Reilly breezed past him without a word, entered his office and closed the door behind him. Tracy looked at the secretary who shrugged. He hadn't yet had the opportunity to be introduced to the big boss. He should have met O'Reilly on his first week on the job but the boss had been away attending a course and by the time he returned the meeting had been put on ice. There was no great love for the chief super in the station. The common perception was that the boss lacked empathy and leadership skills and should never have been promoted into a staff management job. But the Garda Síochána was not a meritocracy. Tracy shuffled his feet. Fiona would be arriving downstairs and she would be expecting him to have completed the tasks she'd given him before leaving the previous evening. The phone on the secretary's desk rang and she answered. Tracy could enter the inner sanctum.

O'Reilly was seated behind his desk shuffling papers when Tracy entered. Nobody in the station had ever seen the chief super smile and it was assumed that the scowl that graced his round face was a permanent feature. He looked at the paper before him which appeared to be his agenda for the day. 'Tracy,' he reflected. 'You're new in CID. How come I haven't met you before?'

'You were on a course when I arrived.'

'Tracy,' O'Reilly said again to himself. 'I heard something about you. The boys in the Park think you have a lot of potential. Welcome to Mill Street, Tracy.'

'I've been here six months.'

'You work with Madden?'

'Yes, sir.'

'How are you getting along?'

'Fine, she's a good mentor.'

'Now that's a surprise. What do you want?'

Tracy explained the purpose of the warrant.

O'Reilly took the warrant and signed it. 'At least you found out who the bugger was. It was beginning to look like he was going to end up as a John Doe, at least that's what the Yanks call it.'

'We're looking into his life now and it won't be long until we find a motivation for the crime.'

'That's your professional conclusion based on six months experience. The boys in the Park have a great nose for potential. What church do you take Mass in?'

Tracy was a lapsed Catholic but he didn't think it was the occasion to declare it. He only knew one church. 'Saint Augustine's.'

'A fine church. I hope you're a regular communicant.'

'I am indeed, sir,' Tracy lied.

'You've heard no doubt of Opus Dei.'

'I have.'

'It's a fine organisation of Catholic men. I'm a member myself and I'd be willing to support an application.'

'Thank you, sir. I'm only getting organised but when I'm settled, I'll take up your offer.'

O'Reilly passed over the warrant. 'Say your prayers and do your duty and that potential of yours might develop.'

Tracy took the warrant and started for the door.

'Don't forget, Opus Dei.'

Tracy left the room and let out a sigh of relief.

The secretary smiled.

What have I let myself in for Tracy thought as he took the stairs. Everything he'd heard about the boss had been borne out. He bypassed the squad room. Fiona would be in by now and he wanted to avoid her. He would head straight for the hospital and pick up the file. A stroll in the fresh air would do him good after that trip to the twilight zone.

CHAPTER THIRTY-THREE

Fiona arrived at nine. There was no sign of Tracy although his computer was on and the template for the warrant was on the screen. The machine would have powered down if it were left on overnight so he'd been in early to get the work done. The more she knew him, the more she got to like him. He was one of those men that gives women renewed hope for the male population. She had come to the conclusion that misogyny was part of the Irishman's DNA. Maybe that was why she preferred women. She knew her sexual preference had nothing to do with her experience of men. That experience was limited and imbued with violence. If she had fancied men, then Sean Tracy would be at the top of her list. If he'd prepared the warrant this morning, he would have gone upstairs to have it signed and hot-footed it down to the hospital to pick up the file. Maybe he'd remember to bring her a takeaway coffee. Her two new charges were beavering away at their desks. She walked to the whiteboard. Nothing new had been added since she'd left the station the previous evening. It was looking likely that she would have to produce the whip a bit early in their relationship, but as they say in the police better early than never. She walked over and sat beside

Brogan. He was on the phone and shuffled nervously when she sat beside him.

He put his hand over the speaker. 'I'm on to Stena Line, they're checking back through their records for the past month. It's taking a bit of time. I've already been on to Irish Ferries and they've drawn a blank.'

She stood and walked over to Fitzsimons' desk. He hit several keys as she approached and she thought she saw a video disappearing off the screen. She knew it wasn't porn. That had been an issue in the past but some tech nerd had installed a programme that scanned the surfing history. That had put a stop to the porn and the emails with the pornographic pictures. It was amazing that the high-tech abuse could be stopped but the shithouse poets and artists operated with impunity. The Sharpie was greater than the computer. She sat down across from Fitzsimons. He was looking through school records. 'How's it going?'

'He didn't start school in Ireland. At least I can't find him in any primary school in the county. If he's a tinker, he could have moved around.'

'Broaden the search, and although you call a spade a spade, I don't. From now on, I want you to use the word *traveller* for the duration of this case. When we're done, you can revert to type but while you're working with me, you will be politically correct. Hard though that might be. I want the whiteboard covered with detail by closing time this evening. And if I find you viewing videos of a cat playing with a ball of twine or any other crap, I will make your life hell. Find out does he have a social media footprint. Do all that before this evening.' She stood up and walked away. She was sure she heard a muttered *fucking bitch* but it was so low she couldn't be sure. She placed a mental cross in the column marked *if I ever get a chance*.

She sat at her desk and opened her computer. Her email consisted mainly of administrative notes from Garda HQ. Thankfully, she was just under the level where budgets and staff appraisals are part of the job. She was ambitious but she knew there was a price to pay. She was scoping the last of her emails when Tracy entered the squad room carrying a tray of takeaway coffees and a buff-coloured folder. He handed a coffee to each of his new colleagues and deposited one on her desk.

She picked up the coffee. 'I was hoping you'd remember.' She took a sip. 'Cheers.'

He handed her the file. 'They weren't happy but the law is the law.'

'The world has gone crazy on this privacy kick.'

'You mean the General Data Protection Regulation.'

'Yeah, the privacy kick for short.'

'It's everywhere you look. People are uptight about their personal data being used by companies like Facebook and Google. These companies know more about us than we know ourselves.'

'I was just discussing that point with Detective Garda Fitzsimons,' she spoke louder than necessary. 'We'll have a full report on the victim's social footprint by the evening briefing. You were here earlier and you passed by the chief super in person.'

'You're doing that thing again. Yes, I did.'

'How did you find him?'

'I never met him before. Remember he missed my welcome meeting. It was a bit weird.'

'How weird? Didn't he invite you to become a member of Opus Dei?'

'Yes, there was a lot of religious stuff.'

'Rumour has it that he joined the Garda from the seminary. He was two years down the road to being a priest when he cracked.'

'Did he ask you to join Opus Dei?'

Fiona laughed. 'No women allowed.'

Brogan came and stood beside them. 'He took the Stena

ferry from Holyhead to Dublin four days ago.' He handed her a confirmatory fax.

'No chance they have a CCTV shot of him disembarking.'

'Shit, I didn't ask.'

'Do it now. That means he was in the country four days before he wound up dead. We need to know where he was and who he met during that time. When you're finished, check the local hotels and then the B and Bs. Glennan checked the accommodation in Clifden for a missing guest and drew a blank. Let's get at it.'

'I received hundreds of photos overnight,' Tracy said. 'I suppose I need to get through them.'

'Crack on.'

CHAPTER THIRTY-FOUR

Horgan was wearing a self-satisfied smile on his face. 'We're making progress.'

Fiona didn't return the smile. She noticed the use of the plural. Horgan was now part of the investigation. In fact, he was leading the investigation. She had been summoned to his office to brief him on the state of play, as he called it just as she was considering her lunch options. They had the name of the victim; they knew that he had travelled from England four days previously and they were working on a timeline from his arrival to the time of his death. So far, they had no idea of the who, the where or the why related to his death. In other words, they were still crawling through a dark corridor feeling their way and praying for a shaft of light ahead. She had received the forensic report from the site where the body had been discovered. It had been thin and devoid of any direct evidence that would identify the murderer. However, every time two people come into contact there is a transfer of some material. Several different kinds of threads had been found on the victim's clothing but there was nothing to compare them with.

'What do we do next?' Horgan said.

It had taken Fiona a week to divine that her new boss

couldn't produce an idea to save his life. She had accepted years ago that promotion in the police was based fifty per cent on Buggin's turn, twenty-five per cent on not screwing up and twenty-five per cent on ass licking. She realised that she would never get direction from Horgan. He was thinking of his pension and fishing. He had already paid his dues on seventy-five per cent of career planning and the only twenty-five per cent he was interested in was the not screwing up. She smiled inwardly at the expectant look on his face and knew that she could throw out any half-arsed idea and he would grasp it the way a drowning man clings to a passing twig. 'We enlist the aid of the general population. Has anyone noticed this man during the last week? Did this man stay in your accommodation, drink or eat in your establishment during the last week? Was he with someone or alone? You know the kind of thing. We need the media and we need it badly. Tracy will put out something on Facebook, Twitter and Instagram. We're getting a lot of photos in from our first request.'

'What about the phone lines?'

'Ward has been seen from Malin Head to Carnsore Point and everywhere in between. I have Fitzsimons and Brogan working on his background and what he was up to since he arrived.'

'You appear to have everything in hand.'

'I don't have everything in hand. I need help with all this media stuff.'

'Contact the Park. They have experts on media.'

'And I'll wait two days for them to respond.'

'Suit yourself, it's your problem, you solve it.'

Fiona stood. 'I will.'

FIONA SMILED when she saw that Tracy was still flipping through photos. She had a proposition for him. 'Anything on for lunch?'

Tracy looked up from his computer. 'I told Cliona I'd give her a bell.'

'I'd like to meet her.'

'You're kidding me.' He stared at her. 'Okay, you're not kidding me. Why?'

'I'm willing to offer you both lunch if I can have a little chat with her.'

'If you're paying, I'll organise her for John Keogh's.'

'Give her a call.'

FIONA HAD BEEN to John Keogh's several times and she loved the old-time feel of the place. Her favourite watering hole would always be Taaffes but Keogh's was a close second. The waiter seated her and Tracy and placed menus in front of them.

'Remember I'm just a poor copper like you,' Fiona said checking the menu. She looked up as a young woman entered the pub and knew instantly that she was looking at Tracy's new girlfriend. Tracy's ex, Emma, had been a good-looking woman but Cliona was stunning. Her red hair fell in curls across her shoulders and her green eyes sparkled like emeralds. Her face had the Irish pale complexion but the features on it were perfectly proportioned. Her smile lit up the room as she approached their table.

Tracy stood and extended his arms. They kissed and Tracy pulled a chair back for her.

'The famous Fiona Madden.' Cliona offered her hand to Fiona.

Fiona shook. 'Nice to meet you. What's with the famous remark?'

'I saw the video. I have it stored with my classics. You're at the top with the guy being interviewed and his child comes in the room in the walker.'

'I'm trying to live that bit of film down. The whole thing only lasts a few seconds.'

'But it's priceless seeing this small skinny woman destroy a big bruiser of a guy. Have you ever checked out the number of likes that clip got, over ten million. You're a hero to women everywhere.'

The waiter was standing beside Fiona and she ordered a chowder, Tracy ordered the fish of the day and after a quick look at the menu, Cliona ordered a goat's cheese salad. All three ordered water.

'You're a camerawoman,' Fiona said as the waiter left.

'Not really,' Cliona said. 'I graduated in media studies at Dublin City University. Jobs in the media are difficult to find so I take anything that comes along.'

'I'd think with your looks that it'd be easy to find a job in front of the camera.'

'I've done a few bits for TG4.'

'You're a Gaelgóir,' Fiona said.

'Aye, Donegal dialect,' Cliona said.

'I was born in Connemara.'

Tracy cleared his throat. 'I hate to interrupt.' He looked at Fiona. 'You wanted to meet Cliona, why?'

'To see if she was good enough for you.' Fiona laughed at the look on Tracy's face and she was pleased when Cliona joined in. 'I wanted to see if Cliona would help us out.'

'Of course, I will.'

Their orders arrived and the conversation halted while they started on their food.

'I'm sure that Sean has told you about the case we're working on,' Fiona said. 'You gave him the footage from the Clifden horse fair.'

'Yes, how can I help?'

'Sean is useful on social media but we need someone to get the message out that we're looking for people who remember seeing the dead man during the horse fair or any time during that day.' She took a photo out of her purse. 'Unfortunately, this photo was taken during the post-mortem. It's a good representation of him but he doesn't look great in it. He was a good-looking man that people should remember. If you were willing, I'd like you to handle our social media effort. We need to hit Facebook, Instagram and Twitter.'

'Also TikTok,' Cliona took the photo. 'Leave it to me. I suppose I'll liaise with Sean.'

'Absolutely, I'm sure you two will enjoy working together.'

'Now, is there any possibility that I can be part of the conversation?' Tracy said.

'Get lost,' Fiona said. 'I want to hear all about Cliona's life in the media. We might be at the start of a glittering career for all we know.' She winked at Tracy. 'You'll get your chance this evening.'

CHAPTER THIRTY-FIVE

After paying the bill which was not too heavy, Fiona left Tracy and his new girlfriend together to have a coffee. She never liked playing the third wheel. She went straight to the whiteboard when she returned to the squad room. Brogan had added the information on the victim's arrival in Dublin and a grainy CCTV picture of the victim's car exiting the port had been added. Although the picture was not the best quality, it was clear that Ward had travelled alone. Fitzsimons had added a copy of the victim's birth certificate and details of his primary schooling which appeared to have terminated at nine. A call to the school had confirmed that the Wards had departed for England at that point. It was clear that the victim had been a traveller. That posed a major problem. The clue was in the name of the ethnic grouping. She would have preferred to have a local victim who had never strayed more than a hundred kilometres from his place of birth. They could interview his friends and relations and form an accurate picture of his life. If their victim had spent most of his life in England or even moving between Ireland and England, digging into his life could cost thousands of hours of research, and she didn't have thousands of hours to spare. One point was clear, the Connors and Fureys could not be permitted to leave Galway county. And returning to England was totally out of the question. The killer had tried to screw up the investigation from the start but he or she needn't have bothered. Searching for a motive was going to be a nightmare. That motive could date from an argument the day he died or might have been festering for years. The central file of the investigation was sitting on her desk. It was bulking out. The results of the post-mortem had been added along with the medical file from University Hospital. But there was a long way to go. In terms of means, motive and opportunity they were nowhere. The murder weapon was a knife. Since the murderer had already shown a level of criminal smarts in the approach to muddying the water of identification. It was logical to assume that the knife was probably in bits and scattered about the countryside, thrown into the Atlantic or buried in a bog. Motive might be developed from the examination of the victim's life or might have been random. The absence of money might indicate that Ward was murdered for whatever he was carrying. After all, most murders have their genesis in either money or sex or maybe a combination of both. They were still playing catch-up.

Tracy entered the squad room and sat at his desk. 'What do you think of Cliona?'

'She's too good for you. If you have any sense, you'll hang on to her but I have a recollection that I said the same when you hooked up with Emma.'

'She pretty excited at working with us.'

'She not working with us. She's giving us a hand in an area in which we are deficient. And for God's sake don't tell Horgan that your new girlfriend is working with us.'

Tracy glanced at the whiteboard. 'We're not moving fast enough.'

'An obvious conclusion for a detective of your calibre.'

Tracy returned to his examination of the photos. 'I'm

beginning to get spots before my eyes. If Ward was at the fair during the day, he was staying well out of the way of the cameras.'

'Maybe he was shy. Although he didn't have the look of a man who was overly shy.' Fiona massaged her forehead. 'Anything useful come in from the public?'

'Nothing concrete. Lots of people claim to have seen him during the fair but there's a distinct lack of detail. We have him in one photo. Maybe this ball aching exercise is our best shot.'

'I can't get away from the feeling that both Maggie Connors and Ted Furey recognised the man in the photo. And why shouldn't they? At some point or other they probably all lived on that site in Screveton. Ward took his car and travelled to Ireland and Clifden for a reason. He must have been at dozens, if not hundreds, of horse fairs so he didn't come just to attend the fair. Would you follow Maggie Connors for seven hundred kilometres?'

'You think they were involved?'

'I think a woman like Maggie makes men do foolish things.'

Fitzsimons joined them. He stood waiting to be acknowledged.

'Come on, man, spit it out.'

'I had a couple of hits on Ward on the Internet. Apparently, he's been involved in bare-knuckle fighting in Britain.' He handed Fiona two A4 sheets of paper with articles describing bare-knuckle fights in London.

Fiona and Tracy read the article together. It was dated two years previously and only made a passing reference to Ward. The main article concerned a boxing match to decide the king of the travellers and the large amount of money that was wagered on the fight. Ward was pictured in a group surrounding two bare-chested men whose fists were bandaged. 'Ward looked more of a lover than a fighter."

'He was too much of a pretty boy to be a fighter,' Tracy

said. 'Given the level of betting, he could have been a punter or a bookie.'

'He has the look of a bookie,' Fitzsimons added. 'Look at the way he's dressed.' He handed over a second sheet.

'There speaks the voice of experience.' Fiona skimmed the sheet. The only reference to Ward was his attendance at a fight between three groups of feuding travellers.'

'I'm still looking,' Fitzsimons said.

Fiona handed back the sheets. 'Add these to the board. There might be a motive in there somewhere.'

Fitzsimons wrote *Bare Knuckle Fighting* and stuck the sheets to the board.

'Bookies carry large sums of money around,' Fiona said. 'Maybe someone was stalking him and they pounced at the fair. There's something of an Irish tradition of knocking over bookies and bookmaking establishments. I remember we discussed a case at the police college concerning a bookie called Dessie Fox. He was on his way to a race meeting at the Curragh when he was ambushed and his car was stopped. His money was stolen and he was shot through the leg severing a main artery. He was unconscious in a minute and dead thirty seconds later. Nobody was ever found for the murder. Making book is a dangerous business.'

'You think that somebody followed Ward from England?' Tracy asked.

'Could be. Or maybe it was someone who was already here. I don't believe the murderer is going to step forward so we need to locate him. But it's a line of enquiry.' She looked at Tracy. 'Get back to those photos. Find me a photo with Ward and either one of the Connors or the Fureys.'

She looked at the whiteboard. Money or sex, or a combination of both, she thought. She opened the file and took out the photos taken at the post-mortem. The bruises on the body were antemortem and there were marks on Ward's knuckles. Had he been in a bare fist fight or had he tried to defend himself against an attacker? He was big and in good condition. He would have given a good account of himself or maybe not. There was the drug in his system. He might have been beaten and tortured before he was knifed. Was Ward involved somehow in the Connors-Furey feud? There were so many questions and very few answers.

CHAPTER THIRTY-SIX

Fifteen minutes before knocking off time, Fiona gathered the team at the whiteboard. Horgan had joined them and he stood beside Fiona after viewing the board.

'We have a definite line of enquiry,' Fiona started. 'Ward had a connection with the bare-knuckle fight game. He could either be a participant or a bookie. In either case, there's the possibility of a motive for his death. His clan might be in a traveller feud or alternatively he might be known for carrying large sums of money on his person. We have to establish what his involvement was.'

'Has it definitely been established that Ward was a traveller?' Horgan said.

'I think so,' Fiona said. 'How is that relevant?'

Horgan didn't answer but turned and looked at the board.

'It could be that some people might think that the death of a traveller would be less important than that of a settled person.' Tracy said.

Horgan turned to Tracy. 'You're picking up some bad habits.' He shot a glance at Fiona. 'You'd be better off keeping views like that to yourself.'

'Don't worry, boss,' Fiona said. 'Ward's murder will get

one hundred per cent of this squad's attention. Despite what anyone else might think.'

'I've been onto every hotel and B and B in Galway and the victim wasn't registered,' Brogan said. 'I'm going to start on the Airbnbs but there are hundreds, maybe even thousands, of them. And he might have stayed out of town in which case he could have pitched up at any of the houses with a B and B sign outside the door. How many of them bother to fill out a registration slip? Cash goes straight into the pocket and no question of tax.'

Horgan glanced at his watch. The witching hour was approaching and his dinner would be on the table when he arrived home. 'Keep at it. You're making progress of sorts.' He marched towards the door.

Tracy waited until the door of the squad room closed behind Horgan's back. 'And our victim's ethnic background has made the case less urgent.'

'It's their own fault,' Fitzsimons said. 'They don't want to be a part of our society. With all this feuding business and their traditional ways, they live in the past. They're always beatin' the shite out of one another and if one of them gets killed now and then, what's the difference?'

Fiona looked at Fitzsimons and Brogan. 'Murder is murder and I don't give a damn if the victim is white, black, green or orange, I don't care what ethnic background he's from, I want to find the man who stuck the knife in Ward's back. Is that understood?'

'Yes, boss,' Fitzsimons and Brogan intoned together.

'We're done for today,' Fiona said. 'We start again in the morning.'

Fitzsimons and Brogan slunk off towards their desks. She watched them pack up their gear and head for the exit. They weren't bad men and they were proving to be competent detectives but their prejudices had been passed down from father to son. The travellers certainly didn't help themselves but it was a mistake to tar every traveller with the same brush. Ward might be a liar or a thief but he might also be a caring husband and father doing the best he could.

'I need a drink and since I paid for lunch, you're paying.' She was sure that Horgan had already given the good word to the Park. The victim was a traveller and had probably been killed by a traveller. Everyone could emit a sigh of relief. The media would cover the event for a few days and then it would be dropped. It was as though travellers killed each other every day of the week. But there was enough video footage of fights between rival clans to establish that old chestnut. It was a traveller-on-traveller job. Horgan had let the cat out of the bag and Tracy had taken him up on it. That was a mistake on both of their parts.

THERE WERE no available seats in Taaffes and they stood at the bar.

'Horgan thinks you're a bad influence.' Tracy sipped his Carlsberg.

'He might be right.'

'I don't think so. I think he's prejudiced.'

'I'd like to know what he thinks of women. He comes from a generation when Ireland was a monocultural country. If you met black people in Dublin, you could almost certainly say that they were students at the College of Surgeons. And, of course, women should stay in the home and not take away jobs from the white male majority.'

'It's all changed. There are people from all over the world living here. We voted for divorce, limited abortion and gay marriage.'

'But a lot of people didn't. You want to see the looks Aisling and I get when we walk down Shop Street holding hands. And God forbid we'd kiss each other in public. The same holds for travellers. The good people of Ireland would cross the road so as not to encounter them. But Fitzsimons is right on one count. The travellers don't help themselves. They continue to speak Shelta and they use it to have private conversations in front of ordinary citizens. And they're not the tidiest of people. We're tackling prejudice and so far we've won a couple of battles.' She took a swallow of her Guinness. 'But it might be a long war.'

'Where's Aisling?'

'She's working late. I've cadged a lift off her and told her that my partner would keep me company until she came.' The look on Tracy's face told her that he had something planned for the evening. 'Don't worry, she promised that she wouldn't be late.' Her phone rang and she smiled. 'You're just about to be released from jail.'

CHAPTER THIRTY-SEVEN

Fiona was on after-dinner clean-up. When they had arrived at the cottage, there was a plastic box at the front door. Given her job, Fiona opened it carefully and was surprised to find two large mackerel inside. She had no idea who had left the fish, possibly one of the summer-house owners. In any case, they were gratefully received since there was no better meal than mackerel direct from the sea. They fried the fish, boiled some potatoes and French beans added a bottle of Sauvignon Blanc and had a feast fit for a king. She finished the last of the plates and went into the living room. There was no sign of Aisling. She walked to the bedroom and found her partner busy packing a case and singing.

'Someone is happy,' Fiona said.

'Tomorrow is Friday or hadn't you noticed. I'm taking my case with me in the morning and heading for Dublin straight from work.'

'Can't wait to get back into the bosom of your family.'

'Don't be catty. It doesn't suit you.'

'You could have waited until Saturday morning. The big event is Saturday night, is it not?'

'I'm meeting up with some of my friends from college on

Friday evening. It's a girls' night out. And I'll be back on Sunday. Probably around lunchtime. I understand that you feel threatened by my agreeing to attend a family function. Nothing is going to change between us.' She dropped the dress she was packing, turned to Fiona and hugged her. 'I would never do anything to hurt you. But I miss my family.'

'Good for you.'

'Some day you're going to wake up and realise that you love your mother and I hope that it's not too late. She's not going to be around forever and if she takes your father back, her decline is going to accelerate. I know you're going to tell me for the thousandth time that I should take off my clinical psychologist hat. But I can't. No more than you can take off your police officer hat. You see a man prowling around a house and your first reaction is to find out why. It's part of you. I know where you're coming from and I understand the level of rejection in your life. Your father left you. You feel your mother betrayed you and cast you into a world you weren't ready for. I can't be your lover and your psychologist. I'm too involved. If you want real help you must go elsewhere.'

Fiona could feel the tears coming and although she tried her best to stop them, she couldn't.'

Aisling took up a tissue from the bedside table and dabbed at the stream of water running down Fiona's face. 'I know how hard it is. I know the pain of rejection. Maybe experiencing it made me a better analyst. I'm apprehensive about the weekend. There's a good chance that I'll be rejected again. But I'm willing to accept that if I can rekindle even a modicum of the relationship I had with my parents and siblings. You're free this weekend. Think about visiting your mother.' She took Fiona into her arms. 'You display amazing strength and courage every day in your working life. Just turn some of that courage towards reconciliation with your mother. That's enough psychology for one evening. Let me finish my packing, we'll have coffee and go to bed early.'

CHAPTER THIRTY-EIGHT

Fiona's dreams were of men with knives and bare-knuckle fights where she was one of the combatants. She came awake suddenly when one of the men attacking her said he was her father. She touched her forehead and felt a film of sweat. She was burning up. She moved the duvet away and gradually her temperature dropped. The dream had been vivid. But it had only been a dream. She took her mobile phone from the bedside table. It was five minutes past three. She reflected on the difficulty of living with someone who had the ability to investigate her mind. She didn't like being vulnerable and she especially didn't like having her vulnerabilities pointed out by her partner. She'd missed a part of growing up by being pregnant in her mid-teens. But she knew she wasn't the only young girl who had suffered rape and been forced to bear her rapist's child. Every event in life leaves a mark and traumatic events leave marks that are difficult to expunge. Her father wanted to come back to Ireland to be taken care of and die. She thought she had excised him from her life. Lying awake in the darkened bedroom, she listened to the rhythmic breathing of her partner. She tried to remember what he looked like and saw only the general outline of a bull of a man who always appeared to be angry whether drunk or sober. The face totally eluded her. After his departure, her mother had burned every photograph of him including their wedding photo. She wondered if he would try to find her if he did return. He was no longer part of her life and having him back might be as traumatic as his rejection of his family. Twenty-two years of silence. Never a postcard. No birthday greeting. But the desire to be taken care of and to die among his own people. She turned and hugged Aisling. Her partner was the only person who could see the hurt child in her. Her colleagues saw only the dyke ballbreaker. Maybe that was her fault. She didn't like to expose weakness and she felt that the person at her core was weak. Maybe that was what had attracted her to the police. She could act the tough no-nonsense copper. Maybe it was time to take Aisling's advice and see a psychologist professionally. Maybe she did need help to tame some of the demons that had taken residence in her mind. She closed her eyes and prayed for sleep to come but she knew that her prayers would not be answered. She slipped from the bed and went as silently as she could into the living room.

CHAPTER THIRTY-NINE

Fiona woke up to the intermingled smell of coffee and fresh toast. She stretched and found that her back was tight. That was when she realised that she was in one of the easy chairs in the living room. The coffee and toast were on the table in front of her and her stomach rumbled. As she bit into a piece of toast, the noise of plates being put into the dishwasher came from the kitchen. 'What time is it?' she said.

'Five minutes to eight,' Aisling replied from the kitchen. 'And if you want a lift to Galway, you'd better get a move on.'

Fiona wolfed down the toast and drank the coffee before heading for the en suite. She wouldn't see Aisling for two and a half days. As she stumbled into the shower, she wondered whether she would be able to survive. She must have fallen asleep in the early morning because she didn't feel exactly on the ball. The case was finally taking shape. Time was of the essence and she decided she would use Aisling's absence to work extra hours on the Ward case. There would be no point in submitting overtime; the staff at Mill Street had been informed that the budget had been expended. Work and exercise would help to pass the time. She dressed quickly and re-entered the living room just as Aisling was sneaking her weekend case out the front door. Fiona realised what a pest she was being over Aisling's reconciliation with her family. 'Need a hand,' she called.

'No, but if we don't leave now, I'm going to be late for my nine o'clock lecture. That is if any of the students turn up. A nine o'clock lecture isn't the most well attended.'

Fiona settled herself in the passenger seat. 'I've been a bit of a nuisance since you received the invitation to the anniversary.'

'I thought we cleared that up last night.'

'I'm trying to apologise.'

'No apology necessary. And forget what I said about your mother and father. I shouldn't meddle in your life. You decide what's good for you.'

'I hope everything works out for you and your mother.'

'It's pretty unlikely. But I suppose I should give it a shot.'

CHAPTER FORTY

The good news was that the Kawasaki was still where Fiona had left it the previous evening. You'd think that a police station would be the safest place to leave a vehicle. But when she was working at Store Street in Dublin, a car had been stolen from right outside the station. Tracy arrived half an hour late and she didn't have to ask why. She pointed to the cardboard cup on his desk. 'That coffee was perfect at nine o'clock.'

He lifted it and drank deeply. 'Tepid but welcome.' He tossed the empty cup into the wastebasket.

'I need you to be sharp,' Fiona said. 'When your social life affects your performance, we might have a falling out.'

'Kettle calling the pot black.'

'Never when a job is on. I'll admit that I've strayed on occasion but it's not something I condone or am proud of. So let's say that for the duration of this case you arrive on time and ready for action.'

Tracy turned on his computer, signed in and opened his email. 'Holy divine.' He turned his screen towards Fiona. 'She told me she'd sent me a couple of interesting emails.' The first pages were taken over by emails from Cliona.

Fiona smiled. 'That's the kind of commitment I'm looking for.'

Tracy scrolled down through the emails. 'Here's an interesting one. When we discovered the name of our victim, I shot an email to my info@nottinghampolice pal asking if they had anything on him. I didn't think that they'd bother to get back to me but I was wrong. It appears that they know of Ward but they haven't done any business with him. He's added a piece from a newspaper called the *Nottingham Post*.'

Fiona slid her chair over and sat beside Tracy. He brought up a piece covering the two centre pages of a tabloid newspaper. It was headlined SCAM BY IRISH TRAVELLERS. They read through the piece together. In essence, the story covered how some travellers from the Screveton site had bought a small piece of land in a village close by for a sum of thirty thousand pounds. As soon as the title was secured, a group of Irish travellers immediately took possession of the site and moved several caravans onto it. The influx of travellers caused a certain amount of consternation for the homeowners in the vicinity. There was some antisocial activity and the peaceful life of the locals was disturbed to such an extent that the local police were called regularly. However, no laws were broken and no arrests were made. After six months of disruption, the locals could stand the situation no longer and they asked the travellers if they could buy the site. They clubbed together and settled on a price of a hundred and fifty thousand; the travellers walked away with a profit of a hundred and twenty grand. Although the names of the travellers were not mentioned, Nottingham Police were sure that Ward was the ringleader of the travellers.

Tracy whistled. 'One hundred and twenty thousand pounds profit in three months.'

'And I'll bet the taxman didn't see a cent of it', Fiona said. 'It's not like me and you where the tax is taken directly from our salaries. It looks like Ward might have had something between his ears.'

'It's an interesting story but it doesn't get us any further.'

'It might be a motive for murder. Show me the text of the email.'

Fiona read through the email. Nottinghamshire Police had a file on Ward but he had no record of criminal activity or arrest. She was beginning to build a picture of the victim. He was careful and smart. He made large sums of money and he most likely managed a book for bare-knuckle fights. Those kinds of people made enemies. There were probably a lot of travellers who had lost money to Ward and thought that he was benefitting from their misfortune. She'd heard that large sums of money circulated among the travellers. That was evidenced by the quality of the cars and caravans that were parked on the Connors' and Furey' sites. Money looked a likely motive but it didn't point to anyone. Ward had met at least one person in Clifden – his killer. There were ten or more men at each of the traveller sites and any one of them might have been the one that took Ward's life. That was twenty prime suspects, assuming that the killer was a fellow traveller. And Fiona knew that assumptions could lead an investigation in the totally wrong direction. They were still nowhere. 'Put it on the whiteboard.'

Tracy printed out the article from the paper and stuck it on the board. He wrote £120,000 under Ward's picture.

Fiona pushed her chair back to her desk. There was momentum in the investigation but the pace was ponderous. There was a logjam in front of them and she needed to break it. She could see no other way than to ask for help.

CHAPTER FORTY-ONE

Fiona waited impatiently as Professor Cronin's phone rang out. Eventually, it was answered.

'Cronin, I'm busy.'

'Detective Sergeant Madden, you said I could call.'

'I'm in a tutorial. Call back in ten minutes.'

She put the phone down and looked at the clock.

Brophy approached her desk. 'I've drawn a blank on the B and Bs and I contacted Airbnb. They'd like to have a warrant citing data protection concerns.'

'Get one. It might be a dead end but they can't fob us off that easily. We need to know where Ward was staying.'

'Okay, boss.'

She glanced back at Fitzsimons. He appeared to be engrossed in something on his computer screen. It would be a real turn up for the books if Fitzsimons cracked the case. She put the thought out of her head. The hands of the wall clock crawled until the ten minutes were up.

'Professor Cronin,' she said when the phone was answered. 'Sorry for interrupting your tutorial.'

'I hope I wasn't too brusque when I replied earlier. My

secretary would have normally taken the call but she's off sick today. How can I help you?'

'We've identified our victim as Dermot Ward.'

'The name doesn't ring a bell.'

'Pity, we have some indications that he has involvement in bare-knuckle fighting.'

'That is interesting. And you want to know what I know about it.'

'Exactly.'

'The answer, I'm afraid, is not a lot. It's a tradition among the travellers. It's a method of settling feuds or of prolonging them. I know that a lot of money changes hands during these fights. Heavy gambling is something that the travelling community has in common with the Chinese. I've been to several traveller weddings and there's always gambling going on behind the festivities. I haven't been to a bare-knuckle fight but I did hear that there was one in Galway recently.'

'How recently?'

'Within the past week.'

'How did you find out?'

'I have a contact. Someone I met during my research.'

'And he knows about bare-knuckle fighting?'

'He's involved.

'Can I meet him?'

'He may not be too keen to talk to the police. The travelling community and the police don't mix.'

'I only want some information on bare-knuckle fighting.'

'That may be the problem. Bare-knuckle fights are unregulated and unlicensed. The organisers claim they are above board and legal. But that's just the organiser's opinion. Travellers don't like to talk to the police about other travellers. They may fight with each other like a pack of rabid dogs but they'll stand together against all outsiders.'

'There will be no consequences for your contact if he

speaks to me. In fact, you can tell him if he'll meet me, I won't forget him in the future.'

'And you're ready to be held to that?'

'I am,' she answered without hesitation.

'I'll give him a call and get back to you.'

'When?'

'I'll call now but I may not be able to reach him. From your tone I understand that there's a time issue.'

'I'll be waiting for your call.' She put down the receiver.

She looked at Tracy. 'Anything?'

He shook his head.

CHAPTER FORTY-TWO

'Lunch?' Tracy asked.

Fiona looked at the clock. It showed twelve thirty. There was no sign of the return call from Cronin. Maybe there wasn't going to be a return call. She was hungry and she toyed with the idea of going to lunch but there was a mountain of administration she was purposely neglecting. 'Not lunching with Cliona?'

'She's on an all-day shoot in Connemara.'

'You two have been behaving like Siamese twins. It might be good to give it a rest for a while.'

Tracy shot her his mind-your-own-business look. 'Are you coming to lunch or not?'

She pointed at the mass of paper in her in-tray. 'Or not. Bring me back a tuna sandwich and an Americano.'

Tracy sighed, picked up his jacket and headed for the exit.

She liked that boy a lot. If she'd been hetero, she thought. Twenty minutes later she was hitting her boredom threshold. Her stomach rumbled and she regretted the decision to postpone lunch. She had been working her way through her paper mountain but thinking about Cronin's contact. She understood the contact's reticence about speaking to the police. It was only a few short days ago that she was accusing the Connors and the Fureys of burglary and antisocial behaviour without a shred of evidence. The travellers had every right to see the police as their enemies. She had all but given up on hearing from Cronin when her phone rang.

'He'll talk to you,' Cronin said without identifying himself. 'But there are conditions. You don't get his name and you don't ask him to snitch on a traveller.'

'Agreed.'

'Be in my office at one thirty. He'll give you half an hour.'

Fiona glanced at the clock. She had fifteen minutes to get to the university. 'I'll be there.'

WHEN FIONA ENTERED Cronin's office, she was surprised to find him alone. 'Am I late?'

'He's not here yet. Apparently, he's been delayed. Travellers don't have the same concept of time as settled people.'

'Who is this guy?'

'Find out for yourself. When he arrives, I'll leave the two of you together and return after he leaves. There'll be no introduction and no farewells.'

'We're not spies.'

'This man's life would be in danger if it were known that he was speaking with a police detective.'

'Do you mind if I infringe further on you?'

'You've got ten minutes.'

'Something has been bothering me about my case. We've established that the victim was a traveller. He was stabbed in the back and dumped on the roadside. Every shred of identification was removed and I'm sure that the murderer didn't want us to identify him without going to a lot of trouble. A day after we found him, a burned-out car was found in a bog. We established that the car belonged to the victim. Why didn't the murderer simply load the body into the car, drive it into the bog and burn it? Why go to all the trouble to hide the victim's identity when he could simply have burned the body beyond recognition?'

'If your assumption about the car is correct, I can guarantee that the murderer is a traveller.'

'Why?'

'Because travellers have many traditions about death and all of them are centred on the corpse. It must be in a condition to be displayed at a wake. There are certain rituals that must be performed. The corpse must have lighted candles on either side of his head to light his way into the next life. A traveller would never desecrate the body of a fellow traveller.'

Fiona was stunned that the point that had been bothering her the most had such a simple solution. She had been assuming all along that the murderer was part of the travelling community but Cronin had turned her assumption into fact.

There was a knock on the door. Cronin stood and went to answer it. He opened the door, allowed a man to enter and left.

'I believe there will be no introductions,' Fiona said. The man who walked towards her was of medium height and build. She guessed that he might be in his late sixties or seventies. His grey beard covered most of his face and strands of grey hair were visible beneath the flat cap he wore. His eyes were hooded and his purple-red nose indicated a liking for whiskey. Although the day was warm, he wore a faded leather windcheater over a cotton shirt and a pair of woollen trousers. There was a pair of heavy work boots on his feet.

'Let's not waste time. What do you want to know?' His voice was hoarse and gravelly and sounded like his vocal cords had only just woken up.

'I'm investigating the murder of Dermot Ward. Did you know him?'

'I'd seen him about but I wouldn't claim to know him.' His accent was West Galway. There were six chairs in a circle in the corner of Cronin's room and he sat on one of them.

Fiona sat across from him. 'You heard about the murder in Clifden?'

'I thought we were going to discuss bare-knuckle boxing. Stick to the subject.'

'We read a few Internet articles that Ward was involved in the fight game.'

'That's where I saw him around.'

'He was a bookie?'

'Among other things; he organised bouts, he managed fighters and he made book.'

'Is that what he was doing in Galway?'

'I don't know.'

Fiona could see that she would have to be more focused in her questioning. 'Did you see him in Galway?'

'Yes, we both attended a fight.'

'Where was it held?'

'In an abandoned warehouse behind the porter shed at the train station.'

'How long ago?'

'Five days.'

'Can you tell me anything about it?'

'I can do better than that.' He fished around in his pocket and produced a mobile phone. He opened it and brought up a video. He handed the phone to Fiona.

Although the video was shot during the day, the area inside the warehouse was dark and she saw that there was a large group of men assembled in a circle. There were two bare-chested men in the centre of the circle with a fully dressed man that Fiona assumed was the referee. The two men launched themselves at each other and as one approached the camera, Fiona recognised Boxer Furey. The men piled punches on each other both taking a punch to get in one of their own. She watched spellbound. The martial arts she had studied were more about strategy and subtlety. This was brute force. She remembered a quote from Mike Tyson: when the punches fly strategy goes out the window. The camera concentrated on the men in the ring but as it followed them, she saw Ward and standing beside him was Ted Furey. She saw them exchange a few words. Furey had lied to her. He'd recognised the photo. The fight was short and brutal. Boxer had lied about winning. His face was smeared with blood when the referee brought the contest to a conclusion.

The owner of the mobile phone put his hand out and Fiona placed the phone in it.

'Can I have a copy of the video?'

He shook his head.

'Wouldn't you like to see Ward's murderer brought to justice?'

'I don't care either way. Maybe he asked for it.'

'How?'

'He was making money from the blood of others. But if he didn't do it, someone else would.' He looked at his watch. 'Time's up.'

'Please, I need a copy of that film.'

He stood up. 'Check YouTube tomorrow morning. Now your time really is up.' He walked to the door, opened it and left.

Fiona remained sitting and only stood when Cronin re-entered the room.

'Did you get what you wanted?'

She nodded. 'I think so.'

'You'll make sure that he won't be involved.'

'I think he did that all on his own.'

'Like a lot of travellers, he's a good man. You should speak to Aisling. There's often a high level of aggression in disadvantaged groups. It's the only way they have to display their frustration.'

Fiona extended her hand. 'Thanks for your help.'

Cronin took her hand and shook. 'I was going to say anytime but I won't.'

'You already did.'

Fiona left the office and made her way to the parking area where she knew Aisling had a spot. There was no sign of Aisling's car which meant that she was already on the way to Dublin. She felt that the investigation was finally on the road. She'd thought that both Furey and Maggie Connors had lied about knowing Ward. She was proven right in Furey's case.

CHAPTER FORTY-THREE

There was a lightness in Fiona's step as she left the university campus. Cronin's friend might very well have broken the case. They had got off to a slow start but they were getting there. Ted Furey must have a good reason for lying. He would have to know that his lie might be exposed and he would become a suspect in a murder investigation. He and Ward might not have been bosom buddies but she was going to find out what had passed between them. Ted Furey had just been promoted to prime suspect. But first, she needed the film of the fight. Cronin's contact was going to put it on YouTube. But could she trust him? She couldn't confront Furey without proof. Her confidence that the case had broken ebbed. Cronin's contact owed her nothing. There was a chance that he had lied to her. Without the video, she would have no hold over Furey. She took a deep breath and told herself to calm down. There would be time enough to worry if the film wasn't posted as promised. The absence of the evidence wouldn't change the fact that she had seen Furey and Ward together days before the murder.

She crossed the Corrib at the Salmon Leap Bridge. The crossing was jammed with tourists and she became aware of the beautiful weather as she turned right onto Newtownsmith and walked parallel to the river. Her stomach rumbled and she realised that she hadn't had lunch. She stopped at Papa Rich's and picked up a spicy chicken salad and a cup of miso then retraced her steps, entered the park that fronted the river, and chose a bench on which to eat her food. Her stomach reacted to the first mouthful of the salad. If it weren't for the Ward case, she would have been tempted to take the afternoon off. Galway in the sunshine was a place to be enjoyed. She looked along the river and remembered the times she used to jump for joy when her parents took her on a trip to the city. They would be in awe of all the fine shops and restaurants. Her mother would have saved for the trip and would take her for a new dress or a new pair of shoes while her father would find a pub. Invariably, they would end up at the Imperial Hotel for lunch and drinks. The Imperial was the haunt where the people from Connemara congregated and once you stepped across the threshold you would only hear Gaelic spoken. She was struck by the fact that there were a lot of similarities between her tribe, the Gaelic speaking minority of the west of Ireland, and the travellers. They spoke their own language and stuck to their own. They watched their own TV channel and listened to their own radio. And they had their own traditions. She felt a kinship. Maybe the travellers weren't so different. She watched the river's slow progress towards the sea. Once her father had left, the trips to the city were more infrequent before they stopped altogether. There was seldom money for new dresses or new shoes. She finished her salad and drank her soup before dumping the containers in a trash basket. It was time to get back to the real world. She thought about spending the night in the city. She could go to a pub, listen to music and get blasted. All on her own. It didn't seem so attractive. She realised that, unlike Aisling, she didn't have friends to call for a girls' night out. Maybe the shithouse poet had realised that and portrayed her as a lonely angry dyke. She wanted not to care, but she did.

CHAPTER FORTY-FOUR

Horgan was sitting at Fiona's desk when she returned. 'Enjoy your lunch, did you? Long lunches are for the political classes. People like you and me have to stick to the mandated one hour.'

'I stayed here over lunch and I had a meeting at the university at two. And for your information, I took a chicken salad and a bowl of miso outside for my lunch.'

'Tracy tells me that you're making progress. Ward is involved in the bare-knuckle fighting game. That's not for the faint hearted.'

She walked to the whiteboard. 'Ward attended a bare-knuckle fight in Galway city five days ago.' She wrote the date and the location on the whiteboard. 'He was in Galway two days before he was murdered. If he came for the fight, why did he stay on for the horse fair?"

'And you know this how?'

'I spoke to one of the other spectators. He also told me that we were right in assuming that Ward made book on the fights but he also handled fighters and organised bouts. He was an integral part of the business. It just so happens that one of the travellers I spoke to in Clifden was a participant in the Galway fight. I noticed the marks on his face at the time and I assumed he'd been in a punch-up. I also understand that large sums of money change hands at these fights. It looks like money could be the motive for the murder. He didn't have a penny on him when we found him.'

'Who was the fighter?'

'A guy called Boxer Furey. He's the son of the head honcho of the clan.'

'Tracy showed me the piece from the paper. Ward picked up a hundred and twenty thousand from that little episode. Surely to God, he wouldn't have been carrying that kind of money on his person.'

'I don't know. All I know is that he was at the fight and he might have had a book open on the result. The man I met has a video of the fight.'

'And you have it,' Horgan said.

'No, he wouldn't give it to me. He wasn't prepared to snitch on his own people. But he'll put it on YouTube tomorrow morning and we can download it. I ran the photo of Ward past Furey and he told me he'd never seen the man. At the fight, the two of them are seen having a quiet word with each other. Furey lied to me and I'm wondering why.'

Horgan stood. It was getting on for afternoon teatime. 'Good girl, I'll make a first-class detective of you yet.'

'Thank you, sir.' Fiona put a hold on using her sarcastic voice.

'How are Fitzsimons and Brogan working out?'

'They're fine.' She wondered, were they? Fitzsimons was a lost cause but there was a chance that Brogan might make something of himself but it was going to be hard work. The contrast between them and Tracy was staggering. One minute in Tracy's company and you knew he had potential. There was a crackling energy around him. The question would become was the Garda Síochána the best vehicle to develop that potential.

'Hurry up and get this Ward business sorted. I'll be needing them back soon.' He smiled at Fiona. 'Looks like you were right all along. The tinkers did it.' He laughed heartily and looked from Fiona to Tracy. Neither one was joining in.

'You shouldn't let him call you good girl like that,' Tracy said when Horgan disappeared through the squad room door.' He dropped a brown bag on her desk. 'Tuna sandwich as ordered.'

Fiona frowned then put the bag in her desk drawer. 'I'll eat it later.'

'Good girl, my arse.'

'He's from a different generation. When he was young, women police officers made the tea and did secretarial work. What pisses me off is that he thinks he's teaching me something.'

'And despite me telling him that tinker is a pejorative, he keeps on using it.'

'You shouldn't have used a word like pejorative with him. The next time tell him tinker is a bad word.'

'People like Horgan and O'Reilly make me think that I shouldn't be in this organisation.'

'Every big organisation is the same. And ours has a political layer to deal with. O'Reilly and Horgan are yesterday's men. We need people like you operating on the inside to create change.'

'What about you?'

'I've already been tagged as a maverick. While I continue to do my job, they'll look the other way but they don't want someone like me at the top table. I had a chief super who was my mentor in Dublin. He was an old detective that I respected. We ended up on a course together and one evening we had more than a few drinks. He wasn't quite out of it when he looked me in the eye. He told me I was a damn good detective but that I'd probably end up as a detective inspector. At that time, I thought that I'd go higher. Now, I hope he was right.'

'And that pisses you off.'

'That pisses me off. I either accept it or I put my papers in.'

I LOVE THIS JOB. I think that I'm good at it. Aisling thinks that I'd do it for nothing. And she might be right.'

'Where do we go now?'

'We download the video tomorrow morning and we have a talk with Ted Furey.'

'Tomorrow is Saturday. It's our day off.'

'So what. I'll call Glennan and tell him to have Furey in his station at ten tomorrow morning. In the meantime, I want you to call the journalist at the *Nottingham Post* who wrote that article and find out if he knows more than he published in the paper.' She picked up the phone.

CHAPTER FORTY-FIVE

His boss's plans meant Tracy would have to cancel his project to take Cliona to the beach. It looked like his keenness was reciprocated and although their relationship was new it was getting serious. It was a dilemma but he was sure Cliona would understand. He knew Fiona wouldn't. He looked up the number for the *Nottingham Post* and called it. The name on the byline was Grace Williams but she wasn't at the office that day but if it was urgent, Tracy could have her mobile number. It concerned a murder, so it was urgent. He called the number and thankfully Grace Williams answered. He explained that he was a police officer investigating a murder in Galway and Nottinghamshire Police had sent him a copy of her piece in the paper.

'I went to Galway on a backpacking tour of Ireland while I was at college,' Williams said. 'It's a beautiful place. How can I help you?'

Tracy explained about Ward's murder and their investigation. 'We noticed that you didn't include any names in your piece on the Irish traveller scam. We got the impression that your local police assumed that Dermot Ward was involved.'

'My editor didn't like the idea of naming names when

there was no police investigation and no real sign of impropriety. The traveller simply bought a piece of land and sold it some months later at an enormous profit. But we felt that the public should be warned in case it happened again. But our local coppers were right, your murder victim, Dermot Ward, was at the centre of the scheme though he wasn't the only one. There was a group involved.'

'Do you have any more names?'

'Ward was the point man on both the buying and selling of the land. His was the only name that appeared on the documents. I asked around about who else might be involved and I was politely told to mind my own business. It was clear that there was someone behind him, or maybe even several someones, but they were important enough in the traveller community that nobody wanted to talk about them.'

'Have you any idea?'

'No, as soon as I was warned off, I dropped the whole investigation. The Post doesn't pay me enough to put myself on the line. Give me your number. I'll review my notes and if there's anything there, I'll get back to you.'

Tracy reeled off his mobile. 'Thanks that would be great.'

'You sound nice. If I ever get to Galway, I'll look you up.'

'I'm good for a tour and a pint.'

He turned to Fiona who sat watching him. 'What's the story?'

'Glennan will have Furey at the station in the morning.'

Tracy did a poor job of hiding his disappointment.

'We're making progress. We can't afford to stop. I'm positive that the answer lies with the travelling community and they could be away before we get a chance to nail the killer. What did the journalist have to say?'

Tracy gave a brief account of the conversation.

'So Ward had at least one partner in the scheme. One hundred and twenty thousand divided by two, or maybe the partner decided he'd like to have the lot.'

'You think that Furey is the partner.'

'They looked as thick as thieves at the fight. He's my prime suspect. Whoever coined the phrase money is the root of all evil wasn't far wrong. There's many a man lying in his grave today because a murderer wanted to collect a few thousand in life insurance. Sixty thousand pounds is an awful lot of money.'

Tracy looked around and saw they were the only ones in the squad room. It was Friday and people tended to start their weekends early. 'You're sure you need me tomorrow?'

She looked at him and he thought for a second that he saw pity in her eyes.

'Pick me up at nine.'

CHAPTER FORTY-SIX

Fiona's alarm sounded like an earthquake had hit her small cottage and she lashed out an arm to quell the noise. The drummers were already busy inside her head but they were using soft bass drums and not the harsh rat-a-tat of the snare drum. She had a scant hour to pull herself together before Tracy would be tooting his car horn outside. She'd known that Aisling's trip to Dublin would be a difficult occasion for her. She didn't do *alone* very well. She remembered reading the Arthur Conan Doyle stories and sympathising with Sherlock Holmes when he turned to drugs during periods of boredom. Depression was never far away from her. While suffering the rape trauma, she'd dabbled in drugs but gave them up. They were part of the pathology and did nothing for her. She knew that sometimes she drank too much but she told herself it was a vice that she had under control. The drummers inside her head were a rare enough phenomenon. She struggled from bed and made her way to the bathroom, turned on the shower as hot as she could bear, and stayed with the hot water burning her skin until she could stand it no longer. She had feared being alone might lead to a bout of grief and self-pity. She'd waited until ten o'clock in the evening for a message from

Aisling and when it didn't arrive, it was apparent that the girls' night out was a roaring success. She contented herself by drinking the half bottle of Rioja she had left after dinner. She knew she was behaving like a lovesick teenager. Perhaps it was because she had never been a lovesick teenager in the first place. The last four years of being a teenager had passed in a fog of lost youth and guilt. Despite counselling that told her that she had done nothing wrong, that she was a victim, she couldn't dispel the feeling that she had been somehow responsible for being raped. She was somehow responsible for having to leave school and giving up her baby. Where those last four years of teenage life should have been about joy and discovery, she'd put a shell around herself that kept everyone out. She'd received the message that acceptance into her old life would be conditional on her putting the whole episode behind her. That wasn't possible while she was still grieving for her lost life and the child she'd rejected. Eventually, she accepted the advice to build a better life, get the education that she'd missed and find a job. But inside there would always be grief for those lost teenage years. She had so much to be grateful for but there's no reset button on the human being. The rape was a door that closed the life she should have had. She had no idea what that life would have looked like. Perhaps it would have been worse than what she already had. Aisling was a good woman who loved and cared for her. She couldn't ask for anything more in that department. She loved her job and could conceive of nothing better given her talents. The rape hadn't stopped her becoming a brain surgeon. Or maybe it had. She didn't know and she never would.

CHAPTER FORTY-SEVEN

Aside from a mumbled good morning, Fiona and Tracy hadn't said a word to each other on the trip from Barna to Clifden. The traffic was light and the radio was tuned to the national station with a boring news programme on the air. Fiona was grateful for Tracy's silence and her mind easily tuned out the drone from the radio. There was no point in castigating herself for the trip into the darkness of her soul the previous evening. She could promise not to go there again but it was a promise she knew she would break. Tracy hadn't commented on her condition and that pleased her. She spent part of the trip watching and re-watching the video of the bare-knuckle fight in Galway that Tracy had downloaded to his phone. They arrived fifteen minutes before the appointed time and parked in front of the Garda station. Tracy turned off the car but remained sitting.

'You have the potential to become a grumpy old man.' Fiona broke the silence. 'I know you had a plan for today and with a bit of luck, we'll only have to put in a few hours. If Furey is our man, we might be done by midday.'

'Wishful thinking.'

'Let's see what happens.' She opened the door and exited, closely followed by Tracy.

They were buzzed through at reception and went directly to Glennan's office.

'You're early. There's no sign of the little bastard. I hope we don't have to go to the site and drag him out. It's too early in the morning to have a barney with a clan of travellers.' He pointed at a teapot on his desk. 'The tea is freshly made and I suppose a cup would go down well. We'll give him fifteen minutes grace.' He poured two cups. 'It's already milked and sugared.'

The tea was hot and sweet and just what she needed.

Tracy took his cup and still wearing his grumpy face sat on one of the visitor chairs.

'What's with your man?' Glennan asked. 'Did someone kick his dog?' Both he and Fiona laughed.

'I screwed up his weekend and he's not going to let me forget it.'

'Did you get the video?' Glennan asked.

Fiona handed over Tracy's phone. 'He may be grumpy but he's a good lad. He downloaded it this morning.'

Glennan started the video and the sound of men shouting filled the room. 'What am I looking for here?'

'There's a shot of our victim having a quiet word in the ear of Ted Furey. A few days ago, I showed Furey a photo of Ward and he swore he'd never seen the man.'

Glennan watched the video a second time. 'They seem friendly enough.'

'That's what I thought,' Fiona said.

Glennan's phone rang. He handed Tracy's mobile to Fiona and picked up the receiver. 'Only the older man comes through. Accompany him to my office. The other two can wait outside.' He put the phone down. 'Furey brought a couple of young minders along. Finish your tea and let's go meet Mr Furey.'

Furey wore a scowl as he walked along the corridor towards Glennan's office.

Fiona turned to Tracy. 'That's what you look like.'

'Mr Furey,' Glennan said, no handshake. 'Thank you for accepting our invitation for a little chat. You've already met Detective Sergeant Madden and Detective Garda Tracy. The interview room is at the end of the corridor. We'll be right behind you.'

Furey pushed his way through the police officers and led the way towards an open office door. He entered, walked to a chair on the far side of the table and sat.

Fiona turned to Glennan. 'We'll take it from here.'

Glennan smiled and nodded.

Fiona closed the door.

Tracy had already taken his place across from Furey and Fiona sat beside him.

The room was like every other police interview room in the world. A table, four chairs, recording equipment, white walls, fluorescent lighting and no window.

'I can see that you've been in a room like this before,' Fiona said.

Furey stayed silent.

'This is by way of a preliminary interview. I don't want to caution you and if you want to have a solicitor present, we'd be happy to call one. We won't make an official recording but Detective Garda Tracy will record the interview on his phone and we'll make you a copy.'

'I have nothing to hide.'

'Good.' Fiona nodded at Tracy and he put his phone on the table.

'You remember that I came by your halting site a few days ago.'

'You came twice, once with your pal and once alone.'

'It was when I came alone. Do you remember I showed

you a photograph of a man who was found dead on the Galway Road?'

Furey nodded.

'You know the process,' Tracy pointed at the phone. 'No nods or shakes of the head, just words.'

'Yes, I remember you showed me a photo.'

'And do you remember that you told me that you'd never met the man?'

'Yes.'

'We're going to stop the recording for a minute and show you a video.' She nodded at Tracy who picked up the phone, brought up the video and handed it to Furey.

'Concentrate on yourself,' Fiona said.

Furey watched the video and handed the phone back to Tracy.

'You and Dermot Ward appeared to be friends.'

'Have you ever been to a sporting event? Some gobshite sits or stands beside you, starts talking and acts like he's your best friend.'

Fiona took Ward's picture from her messenger bag and placed it on the table. 'So, you still insist that you do not know this man?'

'His own mother wouldn't recognise him in that photo, it's shite.'

'That's not the question I asked.'

'I've seen him around.'

'Have you ever halted at a traveller site at Screveton outside Nottingham?'

'I stayed there a few times.'

'Ward lived there also. You never met him there?'

'Maybe once or twice.'

'So, you lied to me when you said that you didn't recognise him?

'It was a shit photo. It could have been anyone.'

'Are you aware of the crime of obstructing a police investigation?'

Furey looked around but didn't speak.

'For the record,' Tracy said. 'Mr Furey refuses to speak.'

'You knew that we were trying to identify Ward. Why did you lie to me?'

'Because you've been running around trying to pin every crime in this area on us. I knew that if I said I'd met him, you'd have zeroed in on me. I had nothing to do with Dermot Ward's death.'

'Have you ever done business with Ward?'

'What sort of business?'

'Any kind of business.'

'I sometimes put on a bet with him.'

'Is that your eldest son, Boxer, fighting on the video that we've just shown you?'

'Yes.'

'Did you have a wager on Boxer to win?'

'Yes.'

'And did he?'

'No.'

'What size was the wager?'

'Two thousand pounds.'

'That's a lot of money to lose on a fight. I bet you were angry.'

'It's swings and roundabouts, sometimes you win and sometimes you lose.'

'That's very accepting of you.'

Furey put his two hands on the table and pushed himself up. 'I think I'd like to leave now.'

'I'm afraid that won't be possible,' Fiona said. 'Sit down, Mr Furey, or I'll be obliged to have Detective Garda Tracy arrest you.'

Tracy stood.

Furey remained standing. 'You said it was an informal interview. That means I can leave whenever I want.'

'That was before you gave me a motive for killing Ward.'

'What motive?'

'Two thousand pounds.'

Furey blinked and sat down.

'You hadn't settled the debt.'

'I gave him a thousand in Galway.'

'And he came to Clifden to collect the rest.'

'He contacted me on the day of the fair. He told me he'd be in Clifden and he wanted to meet to collect the balance. I told him I had five hundred pounds more and I'd sort out the rest.'

'And did you meet him?'

'I think I should have my solicitor present.'

Fiona turned to Tracy. 'Switch off the recording.'

'Interview terminated at eleven fifteen am.'

'I'll have some tea and biscuits sent in.' Fiona handed him a piece of paper and a pen. 'Write down the name of your solicitor and the telephone number.' She turned to Tracy. 'Make the call. I'll be in Glennan's office. I'll tell the lads outside that Mr Furey may not be going home this evening.'

CHAPTER FORTY-EIGHT

Glennan handed Fiona a cup of tea. 'Did he do it?'
'If he did, it wasn't over five hundred or a thousand pounds.' She sipped her tea. 'Did your lads tell his minders to piss off?'

'They did but they just wandered down the road a bit.'

Tracy entered the office without knocking.

'What's the news?' Fiona asked. The hangdog look on Tracy's face told her that the news was not good, for him.

'The solicitor wasn't at the office in Galway but I got his mobile from the message on the answerphone. He was looking forward to his lunch but said he'd be here in an hour.'

'Time for us to have a bite.' She looked at Glennan. 'Care to join us?'

'I promised the wife I'd be home for lunch.'

Fiona finished her tea and put the cup on the desk. 'Cheer up, Sean, I'm buying.'

It was a sunny day and all the tables at the front of EJ King's were taken. It was ten minutes before midday and the lunchtime crowd had yet to arrive. Inside, Fiona noticed a small table in the right-hand corner of the bar was available and made directly for it. She sat against the wall and Tracy took the seat facing her.

'So much for getting away early,' Tracy said when they were settled.

The waitress dropped two menus on the table. 'Drinks?'

'Water,' they said together.

'I'm sorry for spoiling your Saturday.'

'I really like the girl.'

'I know you do.'

'The Fureys might pack up and disappear overnight.'

'You're sure it's them.'

She told him of her conversation with Cronin. 'Two days ago we had a large field of possible suspects. The video of the fight and the existence of the wager that hasn't been settled makes Ted Furey a prime suspect. We have to go the distance with him.'

The waitress returned and put a jug of water and two glasses on the table. Fiona ordered fish and chips and Tracy a goat's cheese salad.

Fiona looked up from the table. 'I think we may have company.'

Tracy turned in time to see Boxer Furey and two young travellers heading in their direction. He was about to rise when Fiona put her hand on his arm.

'No need.' She saw the barman watching the men approaching their table.

'You're keeping my dad in.' Boxer stood facing Fiona, one man on either side of him.

'You're making the barman nervous,' Fiona said. 'If we're not all smiles with each other, he'll be on the phone to the station and your father won't be the only one inside. Send the lads outside and take the empty seat.'

Boxer hesitated a moment before ordering his companions out and taking a seat.

Fiona saw the barman relax and start serving drinks. She looked at Boxer. The marks on his face were healing nicely. Without the cuts and bruises, he was a good-looking young man. 'Your father is what we call helping us with our enquiries. The more help he gives us the sooner he'll be back on the street.'

'He didn't kill Ward,' Boxer said.

'Then he has nothing to worry about.'

'I Googled you. I saw that video of you taking out that guy in Galway. That was a classy exhibition.'

'I suppose that means that you won't be taking your chance with me.'

'I think Ward stiffed us. He set up that fight and fixed it somehow.'

'Or maybe you just lost. Nobody asked your father to wager two thousand pounds on the outcome.'

'We thought I could handle Nevens. I beat him before.'

'That bet gave your father the motive to kill Ward.'

'Are you kidding? We often bet a lot more than that. Sometimes you win and sometimes you lose. Two grand is water off a duck's back.'

The barman, a good solid Connemara man, approached their table carrying two plates. He put the fish and chips in front of Fiona and the goat's cheese in front of Tracy. 'Are we alright here?'

'No bother.' Fiona flashed her warrant card. 'Just a lunch and a friendly conversation.'

The barman looked at Boxer before returning to the bar.

'Your father was about to tell us that he met with Ward on the day he died. As far as we know, he was the last man to see Ward alive.'

'Ward was a smart arse. He'd scam his grandmother. He

made a killing on a land deal in England and was lording it over the rest of us waving twenty and fifty-pound notes about the place.'

'You and your dad didn't like him.' Fiona forked some fish into her mouth. It was fresh and tasty.

'No we didn't but we didn't want to kill him.'

'Then you have nothing to worry about.'

'You mean that a traveller has never been fitted up for a crime they didn't commit. I bet your bosses would be delighted to get a traveller in the dock.'

'Tracy and I don't fit people up. We follow the evidence. If your dad didn't kill Ward, he'll have to help us prove it.'

'Why should I trust you?'

'Because I ask you to. Find out, did anyone see Ward on the day of the fair with anyone else. Don't just throw a name at us. Give us details, like where and when. If your father is innocent, I don't want to keep him at the station any longer than necessary.'

Boxer smashed his hand against the table. 'He didn't do it, I told you.'

Conversation around the room stopped. Fiona saw the barman watching her as he moved towards the phone. She shook her head.

'Be a good lad and head off home now. My lunch is getting cold and remember what I said, ask around about Ward on the day of the fair. We'll let you in to see your dad after we're finished with him.' She speared a piece of battered fish, put it in her mouth and chewed.

Boxer stood and headed for the exit. At the bar, the barman relaxed.

'Do you believe him?' Tracy asked.

'Do I believe that he thinks his father didn't kill Ward, absolutely. But that doesn't mean that he didn't do it. We've established a motive for Ted Furey. We'll probably never find the murder weapon but we might be able to put Furey and Ward together around the time of the murder. After that, it'll be up to us to get Furey to confess. These are some of the best fish and chips I've had. Let's get on with our lunch. We don't want to keep the solicitor waiting.'

CHAPTER FORTY-NINE

The Garda on reception at Clifden station called as Fiona was at the bar paying the bill. The solicitor had arrived and was in conference with his client.

'Thanks for lunch,' Tracy said as they made their way up Main Street.

'It's nothing. The barman comped us.'

'We're not supposed to accept freebies like that.'

'The barman and I were like the good-mannered twins. He insisted there was no bill, I insisted I was paying and he insisted not. We could have been there all day but I decided we had more important things to do. I don't feel compromised. Do you?'

'No.'

They were buzzed through at the station and made their way to the interview room. Fiona knocked on the door before entering.

'Are we ready to continue?' Fiona asked.

The newcomer stood and extended his hand. 'Michael Greene, Mr Furey's solicitor.'

Fiona took his hand and shook. 'DS Madden and Detective Garda Tracy.' She sat facing Furey.

Tracy sat beside her and Greene retook his seat.

Fiona began. 'A recording will be made of this interview and a copy will be available before you leave.' She nodded at Tracy who turned on the recording equipment and did the preamble.

'Do you have a warrant to hold Mr Furey?' Greene asked.

'No,' Fiona said. 'I am holding your client in accordance with section four of the Criminal Law Act of 1997 in that an arrestable crime has been committed and I suspect that your client may be guilty of that offence. Your client is not under arrest and may leave at any time but should he wish to do so, he will be arrested and cautioned and that arrest will be on his record.'

No one moved.

'Okay, Mr Furey,' Fiona said. 'In our earlier conversation, we'd reached the point where you had an arrangement to meet Dermot Ward at the horse fair. Did you meet him?'

'Yes, I did.'

'And was the purpose of this meeting for you to settle your betting debt with Ward?'

'It was. I handed him five hundred pounds and told him I'd get the balance to him within a week.'

'At what time did you meet him?'

'Three o'clock.'

'And you passed over the money and that's all.'

'Pretty much. I told him that I thought Boxer's opponent was doped up.'

'Meaning that the man your son fought had taken some performance-enhancing drug.'

'Yes, I've been in this game a long time and I reckon the other boy was hopped up to his eyeballs.'

'And that made you angry?'

'I wasn't happy. But Boxer lost and I pay my debts. I wouldn't bet with Ward again. I should have known better. He had a reputation as a black-hearted bastard who would cheat his own people.'

'You didn't see him again after three?'

'No.'

'At three o'clock Ward had a considerable amount of money in his possession.'

'He took the five hundred from me and added it to a roll from his pocket. He always carried his money tied up by rubber bands. I have no idea how much he had.'

'So far we haven't recovered any money. His pockets were empty.'

'When I left him just after three o'clock, he had a packet on him and he was in good humour. Honest to God, I didn't see him after that. Yes, I was angry to lose two grand but I'd get over it. I didn't like the idea that I'd been gypped but I'd no proof. It wasn't enough to kill a man over.'

'If I was to take a few guards along to the site and search your caravan, we wouldn't find a large sum of money?'

'I've only got enough to get us back to England.'

'I won't be able to get a warrant to search your caravan until Monday morning. But you could give me your approval to carry out the search now.'

Furey looked at Greene who nodded.

'You can search my caravan.'

Fiona nodded at Tracy who terminated the interview.

'Thank you, Mr Furey, you've saved us a lot of time and trouble.'

'I didn't kill that man.'

Fiona and Tracy rolled up to the Furey halting site accompanied by two young guards that Glennan had provided. Boxer and his two friends had barred their entrance until Fiona had contacted his father on the phone and he instructed his son to facilitate the police. Furey's caravan was one of the biggest and most modern.

Fiona briefed her team to carry out the search with care. 'We're only looking for money, nothing else. Don't tear the place apart. And use your gloves.' She gave each man two evidence bags. 'Drop whatever you find into the bags.'

Fiona and Tracy entered first. She estimated the caravan at forty feet. The front end was set up as the living area while the back end was divided into two bedrooms. She ordered the young constables to search the living area while she and Tracy took the bedrooms. She realised that she hadn't seen a Mrs Furey but she noted a woman's touch in the main bedroom. The examination of a wardrobe produced only male clothes. A search of the pockets found no money. She rummaged through a cupboard and a small sideboard with a similar result. She lifted the mattress and found nothing. She squeezed the pillows but only felt foam. After exploring the nooks and crannies, she gave up and went next door. 'Anything?'

'Not a thing,' Tracy said. 'I think Boxer is kipping in here. It's a bit of a mess and I've found forty-two quid in notes and change.'

'Let's give the lads a hand.'

Fiona and Tracy passed by the kitchen area and searched the presses, the cooker and the fridge-freezer without finding any cash. They moved on to the living room. One of the constables handed over an evidence bag that contained ninety English pounds in notes. Fiona searched for a hiding place but found none. There were a couple of cushions on a settee, she picked them up and squeezed them. Nothing. She flicked through a couple of porno magazines. It was looking like the search was a bust.

'He could have palmed the money off to someone when you called him in for the interview,' Tracy said.

'You're right, he could have. But it's just as likely that he didn't have it in the first place. We always need to examine our assumptions and it could be that our prime suspect might not be our man. Ward would have had enough money on him to cover his bets. That means he had more than two thousand pounds. Add in Furey's losses and he could have been carrying more than four thousand pounds at the fair. We need to take another look at that video of the fight. Anyone who was there might have witnessed Furey handing over the thousand pounds.'

'What are you going to do with Furey?'

'We'll cut him loose but he can't leave Clifden.'

'So, today was really for nothing.'

'On the contrary, I think we learned a lot. We know Ward was carrying a lot of money on the day he died. We know he was alive at three o'clock and that Ted Furey might have been the last man to see him alive.'

'Furey's not off the hook?'

'Nobody is off the hook until we nail the murderer.' She stood in the centre of the caravan. 'Okay, lads, we're done. Make sure everything is back where we found it. Let's see if we can salvage at least some of Detective Tracy's Saturday.'

CHAPTER FIFTY

Fiona was wired. She needed badly to wind down. She had put all her energy into proving that Ted Furey was the murderer and she'd been wrong. She sat on the patio at Pádraicíns Bar and reflected on the day. In order to help her reflect, she had ordered a half dozen oysters and a pint of Guinness. She was enjoying both as she watched the activity on the beach beneath her. Tracy had dropped her off as he raced to Galway to pick up his girlfriend. He had it bad and she was happy for him. Since she had nowhere to go and nothing to do, an early evening on a patio in the sun seemed like a good idea. She hadn't looked at her phone until she had swallowed some oysters and washed them down with a gulp of Guinness. She'd put her phone on silent at Clifden Garda station so she'd missed the six messages Aisling sent. They had varied from a description of the girl's night out – enjoyable reminiscence of college – to the frantic *Where the hell are you?* She answered by sending a picture of the table with its plate of oysters and Guinness with the beach in the background. Aisling had texted back *lucky you*. But she didn't feel at all lucky to have had the case she was building against Ted Furey blown out of the water. She had lied when she told Tracy that

Furey was still in the frame. She was one hundred per cent sure that he was not their man. Where did that leave them? Probably up shit creek without a paddle. She was sure that Ward's stash was the motive for the murder. If he'd pulled it out at the fight in Galway, any one of the spectators might have set their sights on him. They were back in the realm of multiple suspects. She'd asked Tracy to forward her the video but in his rush, he'd probably forgotten. She couldn't find it on her phone and she sent him a text to that effect. There was no reply and she assumed he had other things on his mind. She finished her Guinness and ordered another. There was no reason to go back to the cottage and in any case, when the time came, she could order a taxi or walk. She thought back to Cronin's opinion that the murderer had been a traveller. She could see his logic. There were at least thirty men spectating at the fight in Galway. They were probably all travellers. How many of them knew Ward and saw the money he was carrying? Which one of them would have stalked him, followed him to Clifden and murdered him? Who would have hung around long enough to drive his car into the bog and torch it? How would they have managed to get back to Clifden from the bog? She would have to come up with answers soon. The travellers could not be kept in Clifden indefinitely. The sun was making its long passage west. She felt its warm rays on her face. When this case was finished, she'd take a couple of weeks off. She and Aisling could head for the sun or just chill out if the good weather persisted. She sipped her Guinness. To hell with it, she thought. She'd check out the video of the fight tomorrow. In the meantime, she might find the answers to the questions that were bothering her.

CHAPTER FIFTY-ONE

Fiona had awoken to the smell of bacon, sausage and fresh coffee. At first, she thought it was a dream, but If it was a dream, then it was a beautiful one. The smell was still strong when her eyes opened and her senses became active. The digital figures on the bedside clock said it was seven thirteen. She shook her head and realised she hadn't been dreaming. She threw on a bathrobe, rushed into the living room and tumbled over Aisling's weekend case that was lying on the floor close to the bedroom door.

'What the hell are you doing down there.' Fiona looked up and saw Aisling looking down at her.

'I saw a stain on the carpet and I thought I'd take a closer look at it.'

Aisling smiled then held her hand out and pulled Fiona to her feet. They hugged. 'I wanted to surprise you. A Sunday fry-up was always one of our big treats. And I managed to buy some fantastic sourdough bread in Dublin yesterday.'

'What are you doing here? I wasn't expecting you until later.'

Aisling led Fiona to the kitchen. 'I woke at half five. I'd already said my goodbyes and I told my parents that I was leaving first thing in the morning. It's one and a half hours to Galway and fifteen minutes to here. I didn't want to wake you so I started on breakfast. You set the table and tell me what kept you so busy yesterday that you ignored five text messages.'

'I didn't ignore them. I was interviewing a suspect in Clifden and I put my phone on silent. Then I forgot to take it off.'

'Tell me about it.'

Fiona told the story of the previous day and by the time she'd got to her evening eating oysters and drinking Guinness, a breakfast of eggs, bacon, sausage and black pudding was on the table.

'Where does that leave you?'

'Not exactly at the beginning but still searching for a prime suspect.

'You've made so much progress.'

'Tell me about Dublin.'

'Nothing much to tell. You saw the photos from the girls' night out. We drank a lot, reminisced about college and shat on the men in our lives. It ended, as I expected, in a tear fest. The anniversary went off well enough. There was tension but it didn't boil over. I think there's a recognition that I'm still a member of the family and despite me being an idiot, we all still love one another. I was glad to leave because I didn't want to put the change of heart to the test for another day.'

'I was thinking of going to the station today.'

'To do what?'

'I have no idea. I just know that if I stop pushing, the investigation will get away from me.'

'Maybe if you take a break, some of the ideas will crystalise in your mind.'

'Police work isn't about having a Eureka moment. It's about building the evidence block by block. The nice stack of blocks I was building just collapsed. Now I need to build another one.'

'It's a beautiful day, let's take a drive, have lunch, do something fun.'

'God, who's this new Aisling McGoldrick. You should go to Dublin more often.'

Aisling's idea of a lazy Sunday trip was a drive around the Connemara National Park followed by a visit to Kylemore Abbey. By lunchtime, they had doubled back and Fiona realised that they were heading in the direction of Glenmore. 'What are you up to?'

Aisling stared straight ahead. 'I want to see Tigh Jimmy. You told me that he does a good lunch.'

'Then I lied. Jimmy makes a decent ham and cheese sandwich and that's about it.'

'Well, I'm ready to eat and if that's all that's on the menu then so be it.'

'We're not going to Glenmore for a sandwich at Jimmy's, are we?'

'No, we're not.'

'I don't like where this is going.'

'It's a beautiful day and we're going to visit your mother.'

'The hell we are. Turn this car around or I'm going to open the door and throw myself out.'

'That would be a bit melodramatic, don't you think. Are you so afraid of facing up to the past that you'd risk death or a serious injury to avoid it?'

Fiona put her hand on the door lock and opened the door.

'Don't be silly.' Aisling pulled into the side of the road and stopped.

Fiona faced her 'Turn around.'

'No.'

Fiona opened the door wider. 'I'll walk home.'

'No you won't. Stop acting like an adolescent. Let all the hurt and the angst go. You want to reconcile with your mother.

You need to reconcile. You need her and she needs you. I phoned her yesterday and told her we'd drop by. She cried. It would be cruel not to follow through. Close the door. It's only five minutes down the road.'

Fiona recognised that what she did in the next few minutes could have a profound impact on the rest of her life. She had spent more than half of her life without a mother. The question for her was whether she wanted to continue with that situation. She pulled the door closed.

'Good girl.' Aisling put the car in gear and pulled back on the road. 'We're going for tea and cake. That's all. This is not the time to get into a slanging match. That can come later.'

Fiona stood on the step at the front of the council cottage where she'd spent the first sixteen years of her life. It took an act of will not to escape after Aisling rang the bell. When the door opened there was nowhere to run.

Mary Madden had put on her best dress and applied make-up. She held the door wide.

'*Tá fáilte romhat, tar isteach.*' She looked at Aisling. 'I'm sorry. Maybe you don't have Irish. You're welcome, please come in.'

Fiona was worried that there would be an attempt at a hug but there was none. Perhaps Aisling had issued instructions to her mother as she had to her.

They were ushered into the small living room which was tidier than Fiona remembered. The coffee table had been set with cups, sugar and milk. A selection of shop-bought cakes sat on a plate. There was tension in the air but the stage was set for a civilised encounter.

The pouring of the tea was followed by a pregnant silence.

'It's been a while,' Mary said.

'Eighteen years to be exact,' Fiona said. 'Two more years than I spent in this house with you. You missed all the good stuff. The guilt at giving up my child, the sense of helplessness, the betrayal of the fact that a sixteen-year-old girl was raped and made pregnant, the

descent into drugs, the wanton sex. Maybe you should have been there for all that.'

'None of us is perfect. I made some bad decisions. But you've done all right. You made a life for yourself. You got educated, joined the Garda Síochána, you're a detective sergeant.'

'No thanks to you.'

'Don't you think I have regrets?'

'Everyone on the planet has regrets. It's what we do about them that's important. You never came looking for me.'

'I thought that you didn't want me.'

'I don't now.'

Fiona's mother picked up a paper napkin and dabbed at her eyes.

Fiona noticed that her mother's hands were shaking. 'We're like two ghosts luring each other to a place neither of us wants to go and to memories that we both want to forget.'

'I let you down. Can you forgive me?'

Fiona saw Aisling was staring at her. It was time to change the direction of the conversation. 'How have you been?' she asked.

'Age has crept up on me. But I'm better than most. I keep busy.'

'I hear Josie is thinking of coming home.'

'He wrote that he's ill. It's terminal. He wants to die in Ireland.'

'It's a big country. As long as he doesn't want to die here.' Fiona bit into a cake and chewed. She tasted nothing.

'He wants to come home.'

'This isn't his home and he's not going to turn the woman he abandoned into his carer. Tell him that.'

'He wasn't a bad man.'

Fiona finished her cake. 'Tell him I said it'd be worse for

him to come back here. Let his American girlfriend take care of him.' She stood. 'Aisling and I have to get back to Galway.'

'You'll come again.'

'I will but maybe I'll leave Aisling at home the next time.'

Fiona stopped at the car and turned. Her mother was at the door waving goodbye.

'That wasn't so bad,' Aisling said as they settled in the car.

'Wasn't it?'

CHAPTER FIFTY-TWO

Fiona tossed her bag on the floor and flopped into her chair. The squad room was empty and it would be an hour before the rest of the crew arrived. She and Aisling had enjoyed their day off. Aisling's little surprise had led to a taboo being broken and she wasn't sure had led to the reconciliation that her partner had hoped for. There was a long road ahead in rebuilding a relationship but she supposed it was a starting point. In the meantime, she was beginning to accept the fact that she loved the west of Ireland. It hadn't been kind to her in many ways but it was a great place with kind-hearted people. She resolved to speak more Gaelic and not to be so uptight about using her native tongue.

Tracy had finally responded to her texts and sent her the video of the Galway fight. But she left it alone. It was too small to view on her phone. She needed to examine the faces of the spectators. Luckily, the person doing the recording had panned around the crowd. She looked at the twenty-one-inch monitor on Tracy's desk. That was where she wanted to view the footage. She walked to the whiteboard. Nothing new had been added. What about Boxer? He had a motive. He believed that Ward had been involved in a scheme to scam the punters.

Having already beaten his opponent once, the smart money would have been on him. Nevens' win would have been a windfall for Ward. She doubted that Boxer was concerned with the money. He was an impetuous young man and losing to a member of a clan they were feuding with would be a huge loss of face. Maybe that was enough for him to murder and rob Ward.

She was staring into space when the door opened and the first of her colleagues arrived. They were not a cheery bunch. Fitzsimons looked like he'd put in a hard weekend on a bar stool. Tracy sat down beside her and passed across a coffee. He looked tired but happy.

'Thanks.' Fiona took the lid off the coffee and set it on her desk. She slid her chair over to Tracy. 'Put the video of the fight on the big screen.'

Tracy switched on his computer and got busy on his phone emailing the file to himself. The file had already been taken down from YouTube.

Brogan came and stood beside them. 'I located Ward's parents on Friday evening. They're living on a halting site in Meath. They'll arrive here this morning and they want to see their son.'

'I'll deal with them,' Fiona said. 'Ring the morgue and tell them to expect a visit. I suppose you told them to come to the station first.'

'I did.'

'Good man, they hadn't seen the picture in the papers or on TV?'

'I don't think so. They haven't been in contact with their son for some time. They were on about releasing the body and banging on about organising a funeral. It seemed like a big deal for them.'

'I'll have to check with upstairs about the release of the body,' Fiona said. 'Personally, I have no objection to releasing it right away.'

Speak of the devil,' Tracy said, glancing beyond her to the door.

Horgan didn't enter but stood at the door. 'Madden and Tracy, my office.'

'Shit.' Fiona stood. 'I wanted to view that video.'

She walked to the door followed by Tracy.

'Sit down,' Horgan said when they entered his office. 'We have a senior officers' meeting with the chief at ten. What do I tell him about the tinker's murder?'

Fiona felt Tracy stiffen in the chair beside her and she put her hand on his arm. She could feel him slowly relax. She started briefing Horgan. She explained how the newspaper's article led to the video of the fight which led to proving that Furey knew Ward which in turn led to the interview with Furey in Clifden. She finished with her conclusion that Furey wasn't the murderer but that she agreed with Cronin's view that the body hadn't been placed into the burning car because of the traveller death traditions.

'I didn't approve overtime for that fiasco in Clifden. You should have spoken to me first. We've leaked it that the murder might be the result of a feud. It was the most probable conclusion. We know that they go around fighting and killing each other. The media have already dropped it to page five. Where do we stand?'

'We're following other lines of enquiry.'

'I'll pass the message up. Although given the situation, I don't think the powers that be are going to be too anxious.'

'We've located his parents,' Fiona said. 'They're coming to Galway today. Do you want to see them?'

'Heaven forbid, you deal with them.'

'They're already asking about releasing the body. What do you think?'

'I assume you're finished with it.'

Fiona nodded.

'Then let them have it. Check with the coroner's office

first.' He glanced at his watch. 'Okay we're done. I don't want to see an application for overtime for that business in Clifden. That's down to the two of you.'

Fiona stood. 'Thanks, boss.'

'Is that you being sarcastic, Madden?'

'Heaven forbid, boss.'

'That ignorant bastard,' Tracy said when they were back in the squad room. 'I'm surprised he didn't do the *good girl* thing again. If he had, I don't think I could have held back. People like that need to be culled. *Most likely the result of a feud!* What's the basis for that conclusion? I've a good mind to report the bastard.'

'The walls have ears,' Fiona said. 'You can think whatever you like but you don't necessarily have to say it. While you're in the Garda Síochána, put a filter between your brain and your mouth. Let's look at that video.'

They retook their place in front of Tracy's monitor.

'What are we looking for?'

'Damned if I know. Let's start with familiar faces.'

Tracy started the video and zoomed until it filled the screen.

The camera panned the faces of the spectators. Most of them were red-faced from a mixture of the excitement of the impending fisticuffs and drink.

Fiona concentrated on the faces as the camera panned. 'Stop,' she said. 'Back frame by frame. I just glimpsed an interesting face.'

Tracy carried out the manoeuvre.

'There.' Fiona pointed at a pale face partially hidden. 'Give me the best shot of that man.'

Tracy went ahead frame by frame until the man's face was fully revealed. 'Who the hell is he?'

'You remember the first day we met Maggie Connors? Of course you do.' Tracy reddened and she smiled. 'At lunch, I asked if you noticed the man who pulled up in the white panel van.'

'Vaguely.'

'That man is Luke Nevens. He's Phil Connors' cousin and according to Maggie, the two of them are as thick as thieves. Start the video again.'

Tracy hit a key and the video continued.

The fight began and the crowd were concentrating on the men in the centre of the circle. Then the referee dropped his arm and every eye followed the fight and every mouth screamed. The videographer concentrated on the action in the ring.

'Stop it again.'

Tracy complied. 'What is it this time?'

'Look at the faces in the crowd. Everybody is staring at the fight.'

'So?'

'Except Nevens, he's looking at something off to the right. Go back to the panning section and see what he's looking at.'

Tracy scrolled back and played the panning section again.

'There's Ward and Furey.' Fiona followed the picture as it moved anti-clockwise along the line of spectators until it hit Nevens. 'He's staring at Ward and Furey and he doesn't look friendly.'

'Why should he? Boxer was fighting someone called Nevens. The Fureys are feuding with the Nevenses.'

'I'm beginning to get a bad feeling about Luke Nevens.'

'I hope it's not the same bad feeling you got about Ted Furey.'

'Touché, my young friend. We don't want to make that mistake again.'

Print me the frames that show Nevens clearly and the one that shows him looking away from the fight and in Ward's direction.

Tracy did the necessary and put the two photos on her desk.

She picked one up, carried it to the whiteboard and pinned it under Ward's photo. 'Our new prime suspect.'

Tracy's mobile rang. 'Hi, Grace, thanks for getting back.' He listened. 'That's fantastic. How soon can we have them? You're a star. That was above and beyond the call.' He put his phone on the table.

'Okay, out with it.'

'That was Grace Williams, the journalist on the *Nottingham Post*. She rang up some of the people who clubbed together to buy the site that Ward owned. They took some pictures of the travellers who pitched camp on the site. She'll have all the photos by this afternoon and they'll be on the way to us.'

'In the meantime, let's see if we can find out something about Luke Nevens and his close pal and cousin, Phil Connors.

'You're off on a run again.' His computer pinged indicating the arrival of an email. 'It's from Cliona and there are ten attachments of photos.'

'Brogan and Fitzsimons,' she shouted. 'I need you both.'

CHAPTER FIFTY-THREE

Fiona was settling down to work when the duty sergeant called and informed her that her presence was required in reception. Her visitors, a Mr and Mrs Ward, had arrived. She went downstairs. Her victim's parents, looking suitably mournful, were seated on a hard bench. Mr Ward wore a felt hat over a head that was almost a perfect cube. His face was tanned and lined and his hairline began an inch from the top of his nose. His wife was short and overweight. Her hair fell beyond her shoulders and her kindly eyes were set in an otherwise plain face. Fiona wondered where her victim got his good looks. She walked directly to them, introduced herself then extended her hand. 'I'm sorry for your loss.'

'Can we see him?' Mrs Ward asked.

'He still at the morgue,' Fiona said. 'I'll get one of the officers to drive us over.'

'Have you got the bastard that knifed him?' Mr Ward asked. 'Someone will have to pay.'

'I'm confident that we'll apprehend the culprit and the law will take its course.'

'I'm not talking about the law.'

'I didn't hear that.'

Fiona organised a car to take them to the morgue. As soon as they walked in, Fiona was assailed with the vaguely chemical smell that was a mix of strong chemicals and preservatives like formalin. She disliked the smell but it was nothing compared to the sickly-sweet smell of decomposing flesh. They were led by one of the assistants to the viewing room where Dermot Ward lay on a trolley. The assistant whipped off the top half of the sheet with a flourish that befitted a fairground magician and Fiona's harsh look showed him that it was not appreciated. She wondered why those who habitually dealt with dead bodies had such a flagrant disregard for them. She stood by as Mrs Ward wept and her husband shivered a few times as he held it together.

'When can we have him?' Mr Ward asked.

Fiona sucked in some fresh air. 'I understand the funeral presents some challenges.'

'We need to get his caravan over from England and we'll have to inform the clan. They'll be waiting to hear the results of your investigation. You'll be keeping us informed.'

'There'll probably be a coroner's inquest. It'll be a formality. I'll see if we can move things along.'

'He was a bit of a tearaway, was Dermot,' Mrs Ward said to no one in particular.

'Do you know of anyone who might have borne your son ill will?' Fiona asked.

'Dermot was a lad who sailed close to the wind,' Mr Ward said. 'But he wasn't a bad lad. I suppose you know that he was involved in the fight game.'

Fiona nodded.

'That's where the hard lads play. You find out who killed him and we'll deal with it.'

'That's not going to happen.'

'It'll save a lot of trouble.'

'Go bury your son, Mr Ward. I think your wife has seen enough grief.'

CHAPTER FIFTY-FOUR

Fiona walked back to the station and went immediately to the toilet where she scrubbed her hands. When she exited, she still had the morgue smell in her nostrils

Cliona Gallagher was as good as her word. She had sent more than one thousand photos that had been taken by people who had attended the horse fair. Some had been taken by local professional photographers but most were taken by tourists. Fiona divided the photos into batches of approximately two hundred and fifty and set her small team to work. The brief was to find photos that included Ward.

While she sifted through her batch of photos, she wondered whether Tracy was right in his view that the sight of Luke Nevens was enough to set her galloping off again in what might be the wrong direction. Maybe this case was beyond her capabilities. No crime scene, no forensics, no murder weapon, no witnesses and no clear motive aside from the fact that she knew Ward was carrying a large sum of money. That all added up to a handful of nothing. Now she was zeroing in on Nevens. She wondered who would be next. Cronin believed that the killer was most probably a fellow traveller. But Cronin was a college lecturer and not a trained investigator. Maybe she should get every traveller in Clifden in a circle and ask the murderer to please raise his hand. Would she ever get that desperate? She flipped through yet another photo, a happy family guzzling ice cream cones with Cadbury's flakes stuck down the middle. No sign of Ward or a traveller brandishing a knife in the background. She closed the photo and brought up another one. This was an interior shot of Guys bar on Main Street. A man and woman stood at the bar raising their glasses. It was a classic holiday snap. Her finger hovered over the close button and then stopped. She zoomed into the background of the photo. Ward was seated at one of the tables. There was a plate of food in front of him and a pint of Guinness by his left hand. He was leaning forward as though talking to someone who was covered by the woman's dress. Tracy had shown her how to bring up the metadata. The photo had been taken at eighteen fifteen. She cropped the original photo and printed the section showing Ward. She looked at Tracy. 'Anything?'

'Not so far.'

'I have him in Guys at eighteen fifteen. It's a background shot. There are a man and woman in the foreground and the woman's dress is obscuring the other side of the table. He's leaning forward and I think he may be talking to someone.'

'One step forward, two steps back.'

Fiona moved to the next photo. It wasn't taken in Guys.

'Get on the phone to Guys. See if they have CCTV and does it cover the main bar area.'

Tracy looked up the number and made the call. He held his hand over the mouthpiece. 'They have CCTV but it doesn't cover the whole bar area.'

'Can they make a copy of the CCTV from the day of the horse fair starting at a quarter to six and finishing at eight?'

Tracy relayed the request. 'I'm speaking with the manager. They're just beginning lunch service and the customers are out to the door. He wants to know how urgent it is.'

Fiona's first reaction was to grab the phone and tell him

just how bloody urgent she thought it was. But that wasn't the way to get compliance. 'Tell him first thing after lunch. And I mean first thing. Have him send it to your email.'

Tracy made the request in a gentle but firm tone.

Fiona was impressed. They were probably right. Tracy would go far. 'Let's hope for the best.'

'But prepare for the worst.'

By the time they broke for lunch, they had examined eighty per cent of the photos and had found three containing Ward. The one from Guys and two background photos of him wandering alone.

'Not much for a morning's work.' Tracy leaned back in his chair.

'I suppose you're taken for lunch.'

'No, Cliona is out on a shoot.'

'Again.'

'The girl's got to eat.'

'Okay, let's do a sandwich and coffee at Roscoe's. Your treat.'

They took their sandwiches and coffees to go and walked down Mary Street onto Newtownsmith and took a seat in the small park.

'Are we screwed?' Tracy bit into his sandwich.

'Of course we're not. The best investigations have been known to spend too much time following a lead that goes nowhere. It's a process. You don't hit on the culprit first time round and if you do, you say your prayers at night and you thank God. I was involved in one case in Dublin where we arrived at the crime scene and the man who had just killed his wife was standing over her with the knife still in his hand. That's what the Americans call a slam dunk. That kind of case happens once in a detective's life. We screw up and we move on.' Fiona washed a piece of sandwich down with a mouthful of coffee.

'Don't you ever get despondent?' Tracy had finished his

sandwich and tossed the bag in which it came at a wire trash basket. He threw his arms in the air when the bag hit the target.

'Only when I think the culprit is going to get away. I was sure Furey was our man. The motive looked good and he was on location when Ward was murdered. But I was wrong and I might be wrong again. But that doesn't mean we won't get the bugger.' She stood and walked to the edge of the river. There was half a sandwich still in her bag and she looked around for a swan or duck to feed. But there was no bird in sight. She needed to get back to work. There was a murderer to find and she wanted to be the one that nailed him. It was the passion for justice that drove her. She only hoped that nothing ever happened to take her job away from her.

They left the park and retraced their steps back to the station.

'Process is everything,' she said as she entered.

CHAPTER FIFTY-FIVE

Fiona stood at Fitzsimons' desk. 'Any sign of Ward in your photos?'

'Not so far, but I have plenty more to look at.'

'I'll bet you have.'

She walked to her own desk. Fitzsimons would never work with her again. He was as much use on an investigation as a snowball is in hell.

Tracy had slipped away to make a phone call to Cliona.

She moved over to his computer and clicked on the email icon. There was no sign of an email from either the journalist or Guys. Perhaps she'd been too quick in replying to Tracy's question about being screwed.

She retook her seat and brought up the last batch of photos. Fifteen minutes later she'd finished. There was no sign of Ward. She stood and went out to the ladies' room, entered a stall, put down the lid and sat. She sometimes did her best thinking in a small room like this. But not today. How should she approach Nevens? What did she have? He'd been at the fight and he appeared to be looking at Furey and Ward rather than at the action. It was an assumption. Just like the one she had made in relation to Furey. And just as easily blown out of the water and explained. There was no point in approaching Nevens head-on without having proof. And where was she going to find that? She flushed the toilet, exited and washed her hands. The proof was out there somewhere. She just had to find it.

When she entered the squad room, Tracy was walking up and down in an agitated state.

'Where have you been?' he asked.

'Call of nature, I would have asked your permission but you weren't here.'

'The photos from the journalist arrived. You won't believe it. Bring your chair over.'

CHAPTER FIFTY-SIX

Fiona's heart was beating like a metronome on speed as she looked at the photo on the screen. Luke Nevens was no longer her prime suspect. She was staring at two people standing with their arms around each other on the steps of a caravan. One was Dermot Ward and the other was Maggie Connors. They were looking into each other's eyes and smiling. 'Show me the rest of the photos.'

'That's the only relevant one.' Tracy flicked through a series of photos of collections of rubbish on the site and a barrel with black smoke exiting from the opening. 'The locals were trying to catalogue the problems they were having. Most of the shots are of horse shit and other types of fouling that they felt was inflicted on them. Everything was aimed at making their lives miserable so that they would ante up when the time came. Whoever came up with the idea wasn't entirely stupid.'

'Remember the first time we visited the Connors camp. The old woman, Peggy, said something about the look of love not being between you and me. She was right. But I think if she saw that picture, she'd describe the look between Maggie Connors and our victim as the look of love. Ted Furey wasn't the only one who lied to me about knowing Ward. Maggie did it with a straight face.'

'Williams knew we'd be interested in the photo of Ward and Connors. There was a message with the photos. The locals were convinced that Ward and Connors were partners in buying the site. She's looking into the sale and she'll let us know.'

'Print off that photo for me.'

Tracy made the print and handed it to Fiona.

She took it to the whiteboard, removed the photo of Nevens at the bare-knuckle fight and stuck the photo of Connors and Ward to the board. Maggie Connors was upped to prime suspect. 'Shit.' She stared at the couple. 'I thought it was money but now I'm thinking it might have been sex.'

'Maggie and Ward,' Tracy said.

'It looks likely.' She knew she'd answered too quickly. There were some anomalies. She couldn't imagine Maggie causing the bruises on Ward's body. And there was the question of the burned-out car. She needed to develop a hypothesis that covered all the evidence.

'The photo is months old.' Fiona was still staring at the photo. 'But they're a handsome couple.' It would have been so much easier if it had been Nevens and money. She could either break him or locate the money in his caravan. But Maggie Connors was a different proposition. Maggie wouldn't break easily and the money would be nowhere to be found. If Maggie was a partner in the land scam, there would be a lot more at stake than a few thousand euros. A hundred and twenty thousand pounds sterling was a life-changing sum of money. Every time Fiona caught one of the balls in the air, another two or three replaced it.

Tracy came and stood beside her. 'What are you thinking, boss?'

'I was thinking that I was talking through my arse at

lunchtime when I said we were going to solve this one. Every time we get closer, we get further away.'

'Where do we go next?'

Fiona was about to reply when Tracy's computer pinged.

He went to his desk and examined his computer 'It's the CCTV from Guys.'

Fiona walked to his desk. 'Download and run it.' She already knew what it would show. She pulled her seat over to Tracy's desk. They're faces were close together as they watched the screen. She'd been in Guys so many times that she recognised it instantly. The camera was located on the ceiling and showed the tables at the rear of the bar. Seated at a table for two she could see Ward's back and the person facing him was not who Fiona had expected.

CHAPTER FIFTY-SEVEN

It was a humid evening and Horgan wiped the sweat from his brow. 'Run it past me again.'

'What part of it?' Fiona asked.

'All of it, for God's sake. If I'm totally confused, how the hell will I be able to explain it to the chief? Who killed Ward?'

'We don't know. It could be any of three people. Phil or Maggie Connors or Luke Nevens, Phil Connors' cousin. Or it could be all three.' Fiona went through what they had learned, Maggie Connors was a business partner and almost certainly the lover of Ward. Phil Connors was most likely the last person to see Ward alive, and Luke Nevens was in there somehow that she hadn't yet worked out but it was probably something to do with money. Dumping the car in the bog couldn't have been done by one individual and was almost certainly a team effort.

'Jesus wept,' Horgan said. 'How could such a simple murder suddenly become so complicated?'

Fiona smiled. She didn't want to be the one to tell him that murder is never simple, or almost never.

'What do we do?'

There was a tone of pleading in Horgan's voice like he

expected the answer to fall from the heavens. Fiona half expected him to cast his eyes upwards and clasp his hands in prayer. The answer would not come from above.

'I want Glennan to arrest all three,' Fiona said. 'If there isn't room at Clifden for them all, we'll ship the excess to Salthill. We need to interview them but first, we need to take them off the board. If we lift one, the other two will immediately clean up whatever evidence that still exists. We must arrest all three. While they're in custody, I want a forensic team to comb the Connors' and Nevens' caravans. We need to find the money and hopefully, we'll find blood. Ward was probably murdered somewhere on the Connors' site. We've been manipulated since the beginning of this investigation. We've been denied the crime scene, the identity of the victim and the motive. And we've had to work bloody hard to get where we are today. And I am royally pissed.'

'When do we start?' Horgan asked.

'Glennan will hit the camp at six tomorrow morning and carry out the arrests. Tracy will prepare the warrants for the search of the caravans and site and you'll get them signed.'

'I hope this doesn't turn into another fiasco.' Horgan wiped away more beads of sweat.

'So do I.'

FIONA GATHERED her team around the whiteboard and brought Fitzsimons and Brogan up to speed.

'Okay, the donkey work is over for the moment. Sean and I will go to Clifden tomorrow. It's possible that one or even two of those arrested will be lodged at Salthill. If that's the case, one or both of you will go there and stay with whoever is there until Tracy and I can interview them.'

Fitzsimons grunted.

'Something wrong?' Fiona said.

'Why can't we interview them?'

'Because I can't trust you not to fuck it up. You do exactly as I say and keep your mouth shut when you're there. Okay.' She turned to Tracy. 'Get working on the warrants, one for Maggie and Phil Connors and one for Luke Nevens. I'll sort out the arrangements with Glennan.'

CHAPTER FIFTY-EIGHT

Fiona dropped her bag into the corner of the living room, marched to the fridge, removed a bottle of white wine and filled two glasses.

Aisling looked up from her book and followed Fiona's progress. She accepted the glass of wine she was offered. 'You're wired,' she said.

'I certainly am.' She sat down, toasted, emptied her glass and refilled it.

'I hope you don't intend to drink the entire bottle.'

'I'm thinking of it.'

'What happened?'

Fiona filled her in on the events of the day.

'You can't wait to get at them. Why didn't you have them arrested this evening?'

'I want to catch them on the hop. If we strike this evening, one of them might slip through the net. I don't want anyone to run. But tomorrow morning we'll get them all.'

'And in the meantime, you'll drink yourself insensible so you'll be bugger-all use tomorrow.'

Fiona stood and brought the bottle back to the fridge.

'You're not so much a clinical psychologist as you are a walking-talking conscience.'

'Let's make dinner together, then we can watch a film on TV and have a relaxing evening so that you get a good night's rest.'

'That sounds like a plan.' She knew that sleep was not going to be easy.

SHE WOKE at three after falling asleep with difficulty at eleven-thirty. She was always afraid of three o'clock in the morning. Dark events happened in the middle of the night. Her grandfather had died around three and she vaguely remembered the phone call that announced the bad news. Someone told her that three in the morning was the middle of the sleep cycle and that most people woke at that time but went immediately back to sleep so that they had no memory of being awake. Fiona was wide awake. She slipped quietly from the bed, picked up her clothes and moved into the living room closing the bedroom door behind her. She had listened to Aisling's advice on the wine, the dinner and the film. She hadn't drunk enough booze, didn't taste the food, and she had no idea what was on the TV screen. Her mind was working at a hundred miles a minute on the upcoming events. Tracy wouldn't be picking her up until four thirty. The rendezvous with Glennan was set for five thirty. The plan was to pick up the three principles; Maggie Connors would be brought to Clifden station while Phil Connor would be taken to Spiddal and Luke Nevens to Salthill. Brogan would be present at Spiddal and Fitzsimons at Salthill. That was if everything went to plan. Fiona had been brought up to believe the old proverb *there's many a slip between cup and lip*. And although she wouldn't say it in front of Tracy, with travellers, one could never be sure. The early morning raid could easily turn into a full-scale riot. She did some yoga exercises before taking a shower in the second bathroom. When she exited, she dressed, slipping on her stab vest over her clothes. She had just finished a coffee when she heard the car pull up outside.

CHAPTER FIFTY-NINE

Fiona, Tracy, Glennan and half a dozen young coppers, four men and two women, were assembled in the briefing room at Clifden station. The young constables wore their stab vests and carried tasers. They were geared up for trouble. The atmosphere was tense and the response to it was a false hilarity; jokes were told and the laughter overdone. Fiona had been here many times before. She sensed Tracy's tension.

Glennan and Fiona stood in front of the team for the final briefing and the room went suddenly quiet. They reiterated the purpose of the raid and instructed the team that there was to be no violence on their part. They would arrest three people, a woman and two men. Two constables would remain behind with the forensic team. There was a last-minute rush to the toilet before they assembled outside. Glennan sat in the lead car.

A forensic van was already parked outside the station. Fiona walked over and the passenger lowered his window.

'Good morning,' Fiona said. 'Sorry to get you up so early. Like I said on the phone. We're looking for money and blood. Not necessarily in that order. I'm sure there's been an effort to clean up but do your best.'

She walked to the lead car and sat in the passenger seat.

'Ready?' Glennan said.

'Let's do it.'

The travellers' campsite was silent as the three police cars and the forensic team's van pulled in at the side of the road. As soon as the lead car stopped, Fiona jumped out of the passenger seat and headed straight for the Connors' caravan. Tracy and three police officers were immediately behind her.

Glennan exited the car and made for Nevens' caravan at the edge of the site.

Two dogs woke from their slumbers and started barking threateningly at Fiona's small group. A police officer tried to kick one of the dogs as he passed and it retreated but continued barking. Fiona had reached the caravan when the door opened and Phil Connors stood in the gap.

'What the fuck.' Connors looked groggily at the group standing before him. He was dressed in a singlet and sweatpants.

Tracy stepped forward and held out a warrant. 'Philip Connors, I have a warrant for your arrest in connection with the murder of Dermot Ward and to search your caravan. You are not obliged to say anything but anything you do say will be written down and may be used in evidence against you. Please step down.'

Connors tried to close the door but Tracy put his foot in the gap and blocked the manoeuvre. One of the guards came forward and helped Tracy pull the door open. A second guard removed his taser.

Connors was pitched forward off balance and Tracy pulled him so that he fell forward onto the grass at the foot of the stairs to the caravan.

Fiona stepped forward. 'You move and I'll give the instruction to taser you. No one is going to be hurt here today.' She had only seen Connors once, the first day they had visited the camp. He was a well-built man of maybe thirty-five with a thatch of dark curly hair. His features were difficult to discern given that his face was contorted in a rictus of anger.

'You fucking skinny butch bitch,' Connors shouted but he didn't move.

Fiona looked at the caravan door, Maggie Connors had donned a dressing gown. 'Detective Garda Tracy, do the necessary.'

Tracy stepped forward. 'Margaret Connors, I have a warrant for your arrest in connection with the unlawful death of Dermot Ward and to search your caravan. You are not obliged to say anything but anything you do say will be written down and may be used in evidence against you.'

Maggie looked at Fiona. 'Is this a sick joke? You better know what you're doing because if you don't, you're going to pay with your career.'

Fiona motioned the female officer forward. 'Please go with Mrs Connors and stay with her while she dresses.'

'My son is asleep.'

'We'll make sure that he's taken care of by one of your relatives. If that's not possible. We'll arrange a liaison officer to take care of him.' A crowd was gathering. 'We need to be out of here in five minutes. Please get on with dressing and wakening your child.' Fiona turned to the crowd. 'This is a Garda operation. We have made three arrests and the Garda technical bureau will be examining two caravans. I would ask you to disperse in a peaceful way and let us get on with our jobs. We will try to cause the minimum disruption possible.

There was mumbling in the crowd and nobody moved.

Fiona saw the old woman, Peggy, at the edge of the crowd and their eyes met. If looks could kill, Fiona would be dead.

Phil Connors was on his feet and handcuffed, a taser still pointed at him.

Glennan had already bundled a handcuffed and swearing

Luke Nevens into a police car and it drove away immediately. He joined Fiona and Tracy. 'Let's get Connors out of here. These kinds of operations tend to get nasty the longer they last.' He took Connors by the arm. 'Come with me.'

Connors was deposited in a second car and driven away.

Maggie Connors exited the caravan dressed in jeans and her Trinity College hoodie. She held her son in her arms. 'Bridget,' she said and a young woman came forward. She handed over her son. 'Take care of him for me.'

A guard came forward and handcuffed Maggie.

Fiona took her by the arm and marched her to the last police car. Two of Glennan's lads were still in attendance. 'Tracy and I will handle this. You stay and make sure the forensic team aren't bothered.' She put Maggie in the rear of a police car and climbed into the passenger seat.

Tracy took his place behind the wheel and they drove away. Fiona let out a long sigh. The operation had gone off like clockwork.

CHAPTER SIXTY

Clifden Garda station is a relatively small building serving a remote, scattered population. There is no video room to spy on those brought in for questioning to gauge their degree of nervousness. Maggie Connors was deposited in the only interview room and left there to stew. Meanwhile, Fiona and Tracy sat with Glennan in his office and congratulated themselves that they had managed to arrest three travellers without instigating a riot.

'How long are you going to leave her?'

'Half an hour should be enough,' Fiona said. 'She'll be wondering how much we know. She's a smart lady so she won't give us anything right away. Maybe we'll have to build up the picture from interviewing the three of them. One thing I do know, nobody will crack easily. It may come down to how lucky our colleagues in the technical bureau get.'

'If we have half an hour,' Glennan said. 'I'll get one of the lads to put the kettle on for a cup of tea.'

'Put Maggie's name in the pot while you're at it.' Fiona stood up. 'I'll go ask her whether she'd like her solicitor present.'

. . .

Maggie was sitting up straight and looking at the wall facing her when Fiona entered the room. She gave no indication that she'd seen Fiona enter.

'We'll begin the interview shortly. Would you like to have your solicitor present?'

Maggie removed a business card from the pocket of her hoodie and laid it on the table.

Fiona came forward and picked up the card.

Maggie's head turned slowly. 'You're a mean unfeeling bitch separating a mother from her child. I suppose it comes from you being barren yourself.'

'If you had nothing to do with Dermot Ward's death, you'll be out of here by tonight. Separating you from your child is not something that we want to do. The length of the separation will be dependent on your cooperation.'

'Where's Phil?'

'Not here. I have no idea where he is.'

'Get to fuck out.'

'We'll send in some tea and whatever biscuits they have in the station.'

'Well?' Tracy said.

Fiona handed him the card. 'Give her a call and tell her she's wanted.'

'Do you know her?'

'I haven't had the pleasure.'

A young guard entered with a tray containing three mugs of tea and a plate of plain biscuits. 'I already gave one to the woman in the interview room.'

'Good man.' Glennan handed around the mugs and biscuits.

Tracy was on the phone. When he was finished, he rejoined the others. 'An hour.'

'Then let's enjoy our tea,' Fiona said. 'I have a feeling the rest of the day is going to be a bitch.'

Fiona sat in a chair, sipped her tea and closed her eyes. In the darkness behind her eyelids, she could still see Peggy's eyes boring into her. She wished that she'd never met the Connors. There was something in the old lady's dark eyes. She thought it might be malevolence or perhaps plain evil. She shuddered and opened her eyes. Glennan was staring at her.

'Deep and dark thoughts.'

'Something like that.'

'Don't let it get to you.'

''Someone losing their life always gets to me. It seems to me that the more educated our society has become the more our animal instincts come to the fore. Time was a murder back here was a rare and abnormal occurrence.'

'Don't kid yourself. People were sent on their way to the grave, it just wasn't recognised as such. In the 1880s, there was an epidemic of deaths from drowning in areas where there was no water. The old weren't dying quick enough. The press paint child abuse as a new phenomenon, but it was always there. It was just hidden from view.'

'Looks like I'm not the only one with the deep and dark thoughts.'

CHAPTER SIXTY-ONE

Fiona and Tracy entered the interview room and sat facing Maggie Connors and her solicitor, Rachel Byrne, who when she arrived requested a fifteen-minute conference with her client.

'Good morning.' Fiona laid a buff-coloured file on the table. 'I'm Detective Sergeant Madden and this is Detective Garda Tracy.'

'Rachel Byrne,' Byrne said without looking up from the note she was writing.

Fiona nodded at Tracy.

He switched on the recording equipment and did the preamble.

'Mrs Connors, you have been arrested in connection with the unlawful death of Dermot Ward.' Fiona opened her file and placed the photo of Ward taken at the morgue. 'Do you remember I showed you this photo when I visited your camp?'

Maggie looked at the photo. 'Yes.'

'At that time, we hadn't identified the victim. You told me that you didn't recognise him. Why did you lie?'

'I didn't say that I didn't recognise him. I said he was vaguely familiar.'

'But you now recognise him as Dermot Ward?'
'Yes.'
'And you only know Mr Ward vaguely?'
'Yes.'

Fiona placed a second photo on the table. It showed Maggie and Ward embracing at the entrance to a caravan. 'This photo suggests that your acquaintance with the victim was more than vague.'

'No comment.'

'You and the victim appear to be close. Did you have a sexual relationship with the victim?'

'No comment.'

'Our colleagues in the Nottingham police force are currently searching Dermot Ward's caravan in Screveton. You would be wise to level with us. Did you have a sexual relationship with Dermot Ward?'

Maggie looked at Tracy and smiled. 'I have sexual relationships with many men.'

Fiona looked at Tracy. 'If what she is insinuating is true, leave the room.'

Tracy didn't move.

Fiona stared at Maggie. 'Did you have a sexual relationship with Dermot Ward?'

Maggie looked sideways at her solicitor who shook her head.

'No comment.'

'Does your husband know that you and Ward were lovers?'

The blood drained from Maggie's face. Her shoulders slumped. 'No comment.'

'You're not helping your cause. Our forensic team are searching your caravan. I know that you think it's been cleaned but there will be something that you missed. When someone is stabbed, blood splashes into the most unlikely places. The only way out for you is to be completely honest with us.'

'No comment.'

Fiona put the article from the *Nottingham Post* on the table. 'Were you and the victim partners in the purchase of a site outside Nottingham?'

'No comment.'

'What happened to the hundred and twenty thousand pounds that you made from the sale of the site?'

'No comment.'

Fiona nodded at Tracy who terminated the interview. She turned to the solicitor. 'We're building a strong circumstantial case. Your client can either help us or maintain her current stance. I think she needs good advice. We're leaving to interview Phil Connors and Luke Nevens. Someone will either break or see the advantage in helping us.'

Byrne collected up her papers and put them in her briefcase. She patted Maggie on the shoulder. 'I'll be back when necessary.' She looked at Fiona. 'Where to next?'

'Spiddal.'

CHAPTER SIXTY-TWO

Fiona and Tracy exited the car into the parking area in front of the Garda station in Spiddal. As they entered the two-storey building, a Skoda Superb driven by Byrne pulled in behind them. Fiona flashed her warrant card and asked for the duty officer.

'DS Madden.' The duty officer buzzed them in. 'We've been expecting you. Your tinker is in what we call the interview suite these days.'

She looked at Tracy who was frowning. 'Don't bother.'

'You can leave the door open. His solicitor has just arrived. Is Detective Garda Brogan about?'

'You'll find him outside the interview room.'

'The solicitor will want to have a word with her client. I don't suppose there's a pot of tea on the stove.'

Byrne entered the reception area and Tracy held the door open for her.

'At the end of the corridor turn right and it's the last door on the right,' the duty officer said. 'DS Madden's man is standing outside.'

Byrne started down the corridor. The duty officer was engrossed in the movement of her rear.

'Tea,' Fiona said.

'The canteen s on the left and you're welcome to a cup of tea.'

FIONA AND TRACY sat facing Phil Connors and Byrne. Tracy started the recording and did the preamble.

Connors was wearing a scowl that turned the scar on his face into a red gash.

Fiona opened her file and put the photo of Ward on the table. 'Do you know this man?'

Connors took a quick look at the photo. 'Don't think so.'

'This is Dermot Ward. He was found dead in Clifden last week. He was murdered.'

'I heard about it.'

'And you've never seen him before?'

'Don't think so.'

Fiona took out a photo and placed it in front of Connors. 'This is a photo from the CCTV in Guys bar in Clifden. You can see the date and time stamp in the corner. It was taken on the day of the horse fair and is the last sighting of Dermot Ward alive. Is that not you in close conversation with the dead man?'

Connors looked at his solicitor. 'No comment.'

'You are under caution and you appear to have lied about knowing Dermot Ward. I was hoping that you would be prepared to assist us in our enquiries.' She put the photo of Maggie Connors and Ward on the table. 'Were you aware that your wife was having an affair with the dead man?'

Connors brushed the photos off the table.

Tracy picked them up and put them back in front of Connors.

'Were you aware that your wife was having an affair with the dead man?'

'No comment.'

'Where did you get that nasty scar on your face?'

'None of your business.'

'The duty officer took your fingerprints when you arrived this morning. We'll be sending them to Nottingham Police to see if you've been a naughty boy while you were in England. You look like a man with a nasty temper. The jury will see that scar and agree with me that you might react badly upon learning that your wife had cheated on you.'

'No comment.'

Fiona gathered up her photos. The search of the caravans might go on all day but she would dearly like to have some positive news from the campsite. 'There's a lot of circumstantial evidence linking you to Ward's murder. You'll be staying with us for a while.'

'Where's Maggie?'

'I'm sure your solicitor has already told you that we're entertaining her at Clifden.' She nodded at Tracy.

'Interview terminated at ten fourteen.' He switched off the recording, ejected the tapes and handed one to Byrne.

Fiona waited outside the interview room for Byrne to leave. 'I suppose we'll see you at Salthill.'

'I've only been engaged by Mr and Mrs Connors.'

'We'll give you a call when we head back to Clifden.'

CHAPTER SIXTY-THREE

They were on their way back towards Galway and the Salthill Garda station when Fiona's phone rang. She knew it would be Horgan. 'Yes, boss.'

'Glennan tells me the operation was a success. You have the three principals in custody.'

'We've already interviewed the Connors with their solicitor present.'

'And?'

'So far they're using the no comment response. I know that they're involved but I'm getting worried that it will be down to the search of the caravans to nail them.'

'They're all involved.'

'That, or a two-person combination. They know they're in the shit but they think if they tough it out, they might just get away with it.'

'But that's not going to happen.'

'We've just arrived at Salthill,' Fiona lied. 'I'll finish the interviews and I'll get back to you.' Horgan tried to add something but she'd already cut him off.

'We'll be there in ten minutes,' Tracy said.

. . .

Fiona looked through the spyhole of the interview room. Nevens was sitting alone at the table drumming nervously with his fingers. He'd been arrested at six and it was after eleven. He'd been in the station for over four hours chewing over what might be happening elsewhere. He might be Phil Connors' cousin but they bore no similarity to each other. Nevens was short and wiry. He was bald and had a ruddy angular face that would be easy to forget. He was sitting comfortably and had had no signs of apprehension. She wouldn't say it but her own nerves were on edge.

Tracy opened the interview room door and stood aside to allow Fiona to enter first. They sat facing Nevens.

'I'm Detective Sergeant Fiona Madden and my colleague is Detective Garda Sean Tracy.' Fiona noticed that Nevens had a tic in his left eye. 'Do you know why you've been arrested?

'No,' Nevens said. 'I've done nothing.'

'Do you need a solicitor?'

'Why should I need a solicitor?'

'For legal advice. We'll call your solicitor.'

'I don't have one and I don't need one.'

Fiona smiled and nodded at Tracy who did the necessary.

'Mr Nevens,' Fiona said. 'Mind if I call you Luke?'

'Go ahead.'

She put the photo of Ward on the table. 'You knew Dermot Ward?'

'I'd seen him around.'

'You knew he often carried large sums around on his person.'

'No, I didn't'

She placed a photo of Nevens at the bare-knuckle fight on the table. 'You attended a bare-knuckle fight in Galway last week.'

'There was nothing illegal about that fight. One of my cousins was fighting.'

'There's a video of the fight on YouTube. Have you seen it?'

'I don't have a computer.'

'Everything is on your mobile phone these days. Garda Tracy, show Luke the video."

Tracy took out his mobile, brought up the video of the fight and put the phone on the table in front of Nevens.

When the video finished, Nevens pushed the phone away. 'So fucking what!'

'Did you notice anything strange, Luke?'

'No.'

'You weren't watching the fight. You were concentrating on someone on the other side of the circle. When we look at the camera panning the crowd, we can see that you're concentrating on Ward. We have information that he had earlier collected significant sums in bets that he didn't have to pay off because your cousin won. When we found Ward's body, there wasn't even a cent in his pocket. That's strange, isn't it? Have you any idea what happened to his money?'

'No, why should I?'

'Because you were shadowing Ward.'

'Says who? You have no proof.'

'We have a forensics team back at the camp searching your caravan. I know you think that you've hidden the money where it'll never be found but you can never be certain. Why don't you tell me what happened, Luke? Was it a robbery gone wrong? Did Ward resist and someone killed him by accident? Whoever talks to us first will be best looked after when it goes to court.'

'I'm saying nothing.'

'You'll be staying with us for a while. Think about what I said. Your cousin and his wife will turn on you in the end. Count on it.'

Nevens crossed his arms and sat back in the chair.

'I think we're finished here.'

Tracy stopped the recording, ejected the tapes, put one in his pocket and left the other on the table.

CHAPTER SIXTY-FOUR

Fiona walked out of the station, ignored the car and crossed the road to the promenade. She looked out at the extent of Galway Bay with County Clare in the distance. It was another beautiful day. Sometimes Ireland surprised its residents by having a summer, and this was one of those years.

Tracy came and joined her. 'Where to?'

They strolled along the promenade. 'They did it,' she said. 'They're all in on it. Their motives were different. Maggie wanted the hundred and twenty grand and a new life, her husband was jealous and wanted her lover dead and Nevens wanted what was in Ward's pocket.'

'Who stuck him with the knife?'

'Anybody's guess. Only they know and right now they're not telling.'

'Will you take another shot at them?'

'Another and another and another until one of them cracks.'

'And if nobody cracks?'

'They might just get away with it. I'm hungry.' She looked across the road. 'It's been years since I ate in the Coco. They do a brilliant breakfast.'

Fiona ordered a light breakfast while Tracy opted for the full Irish.

'As soon as we finish, we'll head back to Clifden and take another shot at Maggie.' Her phone rang. She held it to her ear and listened. A smile spread over her face. 'Cancel the breakfast, Sean.'

'No,' Tracy said. 'I'm starving. What's up?'

'The Garda technical bureau has come up trumps.'

Tracy reluctantly called the waitress over.

NEVENS WAS in the cells and Fiona had him brought back to the interview room. There was a look of surprise on his face when he saw the two detectives already sitting at the table.

'Sorry we're back so soon, Luke,' Fiona said. 'There's been a development.'

Nevens sat and folded his arms. The tic was working overtime.

'I think you should take the offer of a solicitor. We'll call one for you.'

'I'm innocent.' Nevens' voice shook.

'Take the solicitor,' Fiona said.

Nevens nodded his head.

'Detective Garda Tracy, would you please do the honours.'

Tracy stood. 'Luke Nevens, I am arresting you in connection with the unlawful murder of Dermot Ward. You do not have to say anything when questioned but anything you do say will be taken down and may be used in evidence.'

AN HOUR LATER, they were back in the interview room. Nevens had spent fifteen minutes in conference with his solicitor.

Tracy did the necessary and had the solicitor introduce himself.

'Luke, a short while ago, I was contacted by the head of the forensic team we left at the camp.' She opened her file and took out a page. 'This is a photo I've been sent.' She placed the page on the table. 'How did you come by such a large sum of money?'

Nevens looked closely at the photo and blanched. 'It's my life's savings.'

Fiona took out a second page and put it on the table. 'This is a blow-up of the photo I've just shown you. Do you see the small dark stain on the left-hand corner?'

Nevens nodded.

'Say yes for the recording,' Tracy said.

'Yes,' Nevens said.

'That has been identified as blood and since the money came from Dermot Ward, I fancy we're going to match it to him. We'll check the bills for fingerprints. Whose fingerprints do you think we'll find? Can you explain how you came into possession of a large sum of money with Ward's blood and fingerprints on it?'

'No comment.'

'I know you're not in this alone but you are definitely going down. Now that we have physical evidence, we'll build a case against you. Your best move is to tell us what happened.'

'No comment.'

Fiona looked at the solicitor. 'The station sergeant will be drawing up a charge sheet against Mr Nevens for the murder of Dermot Ward later today. It will be a preliminary charge sheet that we may add to later. Mr Nevens will be placed in the cells and you can make a bail application. However, since Mr Nevens is a member of the travelling community, he may be considered a flight risk. But that's not our business.'

Tracy turned off the recording and handed a tape to the solicitor.

'You're an eejit, Luke,' Fiona said. 'You'll go down. Personally, I don't care. For me, it's a result. But the others will skate.

CHAPTER SIXTY-FIVE

Fiona contemplated returning to Clifden for another shot at Maggie but instead went back to Mill Street. Tracy picked up sandwiches and coffees and they sat together in the small room that passed for a canteen.

'It's a result but you don't look happy.' Tracy bit into his sandwich.

Fiona hadn't opened the paper surrounding her sandwich. She was hungry but she didn't want to eat. 'They're all in it. Nevens will probably turn out to be the fall guy but Maggie and Phil Connors were part of it.'

'You're always preaching about the fact that we can't always put the culprits away. We win some and we lose some. In the last couple of weeks we busted a burglary gang and we solved a murder. I'd say that we've done well. Are you going to eat that sandwich?'

Fiona pushed her sandwich across to him. There had to be something she'd missed. She looked at her phone. Nothing further from the techs. There had to be a murder site and a murder weapon. They could throw away the knife or bury it but they couldn't throw away the site. She and Tracy had done their job. The forensic team had nailed Nevens.

The door opened and Horgan stuck his head in. 'This is where you're hiding.'

'We've been up half the night,' Fiona said. 'And we're only now catching up on our breakfast.'

'But you got your man.'

'We got one of our men. The Connors might slip the net.'

'I already passed the message upstairs and I was thinking of organising a drink this evening for your team.'

'I'd prefer if you didn't. I'm pissed about the Connors.' She picked up her coffee cup, drained it and tossed it into a waste basket. 'Is Brogan still in Spiddal?'

'No,' Horgan said. 'I just saw him in the squad room.'

'What's up, boss?' Tracy said. 'I've seen that look before.'

'I don't like it,' Fiona said. 'Forensics haven't been back to us confirming either the Connors' or Nevens' caravans as the crime scene. We know that Ward was with Phil Connors at seven o'clock in the evening. Where did they go? If it wasn't the campsite, where was it? It would have been getting late. Was Ward travelling back to Galway? I doubt it. Clifden was crawling with people, they weren't killing Ward there. If my hypothesis about the motive is correct, Phil would have been looking for somewhere quiet. Somewhere away from prying eyes. Where the hell was Ward staying?'

Fiona stood and left the room. Tracy wolfed down the remains of her sandwich and followed her.

Brogan was sitting at his desk.

She walked over to him. 'You were working on where Ward was staying in Galway and Clifden.'

'Yes, I have no idea where he was staying in Galway.'

'What about Clifden?'

'There are only two big hotels in the town and he wasn't staying at either. I was checking the B and Bs. The locals are sure he wasn't staying there.'

'Forget it, he wasn't in a B and B. Is there any agency that rents cottages by the day?'

'Most of them want three days as a minimum.'

'Ward was staying in either an apartment or a cottage. How do we find out where?'

'If he stayed in Clifden, the market is small.'

'Get on it. Where the hell is Fitzsimons?'

'Still in Salthill, I think,' Brogan said.

She turned to Tracy. 'Get him back here. All hands to the pumps. We ring everyone with a cottage or apartment to rent in the Clifden area. Brogan will make a list and we'll work from it. I'll call the forensic team and tell them not to leave Clifden.'

CHAPTER SIXTY-SIX

Cleggan, a fishing village ten kilometres north-west of Clifden at the head of Cleggan Bay, is a quiet, laid-back, remote area with holiday cottages and summer homes spread throughout the area surrounding the village.

Two police cars and a Garda technical bureau van drew up outside a small stone-clad cottage four hundred metres short of the village. They pulled in off the main road taking care to avoid the twenty-metre driveway that led to the cottage.

Fiona was first out of the car and went to meet a man standing at the point where the drive and the main road met. She had her warrant card out. 'Detective Sergeant Madden, we spoke on the phone.'

'Fergus Grealish, I look after the cottage for the owners.'

'You said that the cottage hasn't been occupied since Dermot Ward left.'

'I don't think he ever stayed here. He picked up the key the day of the horse fair in Clifden but nobody has seen hide nor hair of him since.

'Let's get in.' Fiona pointed out to Tracy the tyre tracks on the ground leading to the door. 'Get forensics to make an impression. I bet they fit the burned-out car.'

Grealish opened the door and stood aside to allow Fiona to enter.

Fiona's nose twitched at the overpowering stench of ammonia. Someone had been on a cleaning spree and she was sure it wasn't Dermot Ward. She looked at Grealish. 'You cleaned the place?'

'We have a lady who cleans between rentals but this is the way she found it. The bed hadn't even been slept in.'

Fiona backed out and took Grealish with her. The forensic team were unloading equipment. She called the team leader forward. 'The place has been cleaned within an inch of its life. Somebody has made it difficult for you. The pathologist said that there would have been a lot of blood so find me some. I'm certain this is a murder scene and I'm depending on you to prove it.'

The team leader nodded. 'If there's anything here, we'll find it.'

'My partner and I will be down the road at a place called Olivers. Call me when you find something interesting.'

'Where do you put it?' Fiona had watched Tracy put away a bowl of chowder, a dozen oysters and a prawn sandwich. They were sitting in a local eatery on the edge of Cleggan Harbour.

Tracy wiped his mouth with his serviette. 'I must bring Cliona out here. I might even rent a place for the weekend but I might avoid that cottage back there.'

'Afraid that the ghost of Dermot Ward might interrupt your nocturnal goings-on?'

'Something like that. You're sure he was killed there?'

'I've never been more certain of anything in my life. Up to a while ago, I thought that we were dealing with someone who was capable of screwing with us. Now I can see that they're just a bunch of amateurs. The bog where the car was found was halfway back to Clifden. There was no plan. Everything happened on the hoof. They did a good job of hiding Ward's identity. I'm sure the plan was to be far away by the time we put a name to the corpse. But we caught a few breaks along the way. Mainly the fight between Phil Connors and Ted Furey. If Phil had a brain, he would have laid low until he was away. But I suppose a feud is a feud.'

They paid their bill and walked down to the pier. A fishing boat was arriving and as soon as it was tied up, Fiona negotiated through Gaelic for two kilos of prawns. She reckoned that she wouldn't be home for dinner but they would keep until tomorrow and they would be in the way of a peace offering to Aisling. They walked along the pier until they came to the office of the ferry to Boffin Island.

'I'm definitely coming here again,' Tracy said. 'You're so lucky to come from a place like this. I envy you.'

'Envy away.' Fiona stared out across the Atlantic at Boffin Island. She'd never been there but like Tracy, she'd decided the first chance she had she'd take Aisling along. She was enjoying the view when her phone rang. She swiped to answer and put the phone to her ear.

FIONA AND TRACY stood in the living room of the cottage. They were wearing overshoes and gloves. The floor in one corner was lit up where Luminol had been sprayed. They would have to establish that the blood was a match to Ward but someone had been killed in that room.

The forensic team leader stood beside them. 'We found several good prints. We'll try to match them with your suspects when we get back. It'll take the rest of today and most of tomorrow to process the other rooms. We'll have to check out the plumbing. They cleaned up a lot of blood and they must have dumped it somewhere.'

Tracy went into the kitchen and looked around. 'Boss,' he called.

Fiona stood beside him and followed his gaze. There was a wooden block sitting on the draining board with slots for five knives but only four were present. The biggest knife was missing.

'Looks like we know where the murder weapon came from,' Tracy said.

Fiona went back into the living room. She walked to the head of the technical team. 'See if there are any prints on the wooden block holding the knives.'

'Already done. We have a couple of good prints.'

'Thanks,' Fiona said. 'You've done a great job. Tracy and I need to be somewhere.'

'I understand.'

She turned to Tracy. 'Call Ms Byrne. She's needed in Clifden.'

CHAPTER SIXTY-SEVEN

Fiona used the dead time waiting for the solicitor to call Horgan and inform him that they had found the crime scene and that there might be enough evidence to move against all three. They arrested Maggie Connors for murder

'You look tired,' Glennan told her.

'You're not looking so bright yourself. It's been a tough week for all of us.'

'We probably won't see another murder for the next ten years.'

'Don't bet on it. This country is changing out of all recognition. I never imagined that I'd work on a case where drug dealers killed a seventeen-year-old boy and cut him up in pieces to send a message to his boss. The drugs are already here. The violence will follow.'

'A young guard stuck his head around the door. 'The solicitor's arrived.'

'We'd best get on with this,' Fiona said.

'You'll be transferring her to Galway,' Glennan said.

'Tomorrow. She'll be your guest for the night.'

. . .

Maggie's clothes had been taken and bagged and she'd been given T-shirt and sweatpants. Her solicitor sat beside her. Neither of them looked particularly happy.

Fiona and Tracy took their seats and Tracy started the equipment and did the preamble to initiate the interview.

'It's over, Maggie,' Fiona said. 'We found the cottage in Cleggan, or should I say the crime scene,' Fiona said. 'It's being processed as we speak. It must have been a bloody mess. There'll be enough evidence to put you, your husband and his cousin away. I think now would be a good time to forget the *no comment* bullshit. I should add that Nevens had Ward's money hidden in his caravan and it's spotted with blood. You could say that the gig is well and truly up. Do you wish to make a statement?'

Maggie looked at her solicitor who nodded.

'I had nothing to do with the murder.'

'We have your clothes. If you were in contact with the deceased, there would be transfer from you to him and him to you. That might conflict with your assertion.'

'We had sex earlier in the day with our clothes on.'

'That would account for transfer.'

'Phil saw Dermot leaving the caravan. He knew we'd had a thing in England and I'd sworn that it wouldn't happen again. But I lied. Dermot and I were lovers. Dermot followed us to Clifden and wanted me to leave Phil. We had the money and he planned a life together. I was thinking about it. I told Phil I'd had sex with Dermot and he lost the plot. He met Dermot at a pub in town where Dermot was having a meal. Phil suggested they talk it out somewhere quiet. Dermot bought a few bottles and they went to the cottage in Cleggan. Phil texted Nevens on the way.'

'So you weren't there when Dermot was murdered?'

'No, they called me when it was over and I helped them clean the place.'

'Which one of them murdered Dermot?'

'I don't know. I wasn't there.'

'But they told you what happened?'

'Phil told me they were having a few drinks and an argument started.'

'You want us to believe that you helped clean up your lover's blood. The man you had sex with earlier in the day and you didn't ask who killed him.'

'I thought I would be better off if I didn't know.'

'You're currently charged with murder. Did you think that you would be less guilty if you didn't know what happened? You and Ward were partners in a land deal in England that made a profit of a hundred and twenty thousand pounds. What happens to the money now that he's dead?'

'We signed some papers. I have a copy somewhere.'

'You impeded a police investigation.'

'My husband threatened to kill me if I helped you.'

'And you thought him capable of doing that?'

'I know he's capable of it.'

'A bad ending for the raggle-taggle gypsy romance story.'

'No life is perfect.'

'Who dumped the body?'

'Phil and his cousin.'

'And the car?'

'Phil and Luke.'

'We'll get a statement typed up and you can sign it.'

'Okay, what about my children?'

'Your solicitor can handle that. You'll be here tonight and we'll transfer you to Galway tomorrow. We'll have to discuss with the DPP exactly what charges they want to bring against you.' She nodded at Tracy.

He closed the interview and handed Byrne a tape.

'I think there's a lot more to Dermot Ward's death than your story,' Fiona said. 'But I suppose you've had time to discuss the situation with your husband. I wonder what he'll tell me when I interview him.'

'I have no idea.'

'I think you're a consummate liar, Maggie. And I think you're the brains behind the murder. I think you schemed it all. I don't think that Ward knew he was putting himself in danger when he hooked up with you. And I don't think your husband and his cousin knew they were part of the plan. They'll go down and Tracy and I will get a slap on the back. You'll tell your story and most likely shed a couple of tears. You'll get three years for the clean-up with the last year suspended and you'll be out in a year. And I bet those documents you signed will make you the sole owner of the hundred and twenty thousand.'

'If that's what you think, I hope you can prove it.'

'You've manipulated three men. I hope you feel proud.'

'You and I are not so different. Peggy told me she did your tarot cards. You hold a dark secret involving a death. You're responsible for someone's death. Maybe you'll be in my place sometime in the future.'

Not if I can help it, Fiona thought.

CHAPTER SIXTY-EIGHT

Horgan tipped his chair back and stared at Fiona and Tracy. 'The boys in the Park aren't going to like it.'

'My heart goes out to them,' Fiona said. 'It's a result.'

'But not a clean-cut one. Who killed Ward?'

'Like I said, your guess is as good as mine. If I were a betting woman, I'd say that if we located the murder weapon, we'd probably find Nevens' fingerprints on it. That's if the knife hasn't been wiped clean.'

'And there's no chance of finding the knife?'

'Glennan has his lads searching the area around the cottage. If Nevens is stupid, and that's a possibility, he tossed it in the vicinity. But he and Conners visited the bog and I can testify from personal experience that the area is littered with bog holes. If it was dumped in any one of them, it won't be seen again in our lifetime.'

'One of them will flip.'

'Tracy and I will take another run at them tomorrow and the day after that. And, as you say, one of them might flip. But if I've learned anything about travelers during this investigation, it's that they have a code by which they live and part of the code is not to inform on one another. We may have to be happy with what we've got.'

'Conners and Nevens go down for manslaughter and the woman for accessory after the fact.'

'I'll try to tag-on impeding a police enquiry but it's unlikely that the DPP will go along.'

'I think the head buck cats in the Park might buy that as a result. But you have a face on you that would curdle milk.'

'I think we've all been had by someone who thinks she's smarter than the whole lot of us. Maggie Conners set the events of last week in motion months ago. The affair with Ward, his trip to Ireland, Phil's jealousy. Nevens lust for money.'

'But you can't prove any of it.'

Fiona shook her head. She normally never knew when she was beaten. But she had to give it to the witch.

Horgan flipped his chair forward. 'A couple of years ago a visit from the heavy mob and a few cracks in the skull would have loosened their tongue. But sadly, that day is gone. The soft policing approach doesn't work on to-days' hardened criminals.'

Fiona looked at Tracy and smiled. 'You're right there, boss. Bring back the heavy mob. The only problem is that the judges are devils for throwing out confessions that are obtained by the use of the rubber hose.'

'Are you being sarcastic, Madden?'

'No, boss, I'm as frustrated as you.'

'I'll pass the word upstairs that the pair of you have done a bloody fine job.'

'Thank you, sir.' Fiona said and kicked Tracy's leg.

'Yes, thank you, sir,' Tracy said.

Horgan looked at Tracy. 'It's another feather in your cap.'

Fiona wondered why it wasn't a feather in her cap. But she already knew the answer to that.

'I'm standing a round of drinks in Blake's at half five,' Horgan said. 'The whole of CID is invited.'

Fiona was about to speak when Horgan cut her off. 'No excuses.

WHEN FIONA and Tracy entered Blake's in Eglington Street, Brogan and Fitzsimons and a coterie of officers from Mills Street were already at the bar with pints in their hands. Horgan was standing in the center of his troops accepting the plaudits for his excellent leadership. Fiona steered Tracy to the side of the group. 'Don't you leave my side. And don't forget you're driving me home this evening, soon.' She caught the barman's eye and ordered herself a pint of Guinness and Tracy a diet something or other.

Brogan detached himself from the bar and approached her. 'I just wanted to tell you that I enjoyed working with you.' He touched his glass to hers.

Fiona raised her glass before taking a sip. 'Does that mean that you don't believe all you read about me scribbled on the toilet wall by some mindless idiot.

Brogan coloured. 'You're a damn fine detective. I wish there were more like you.'

'Thanks,' she said. 'You're not so bad yourself. If the occasion requires it, we'll work together again.'

Brogan smiled and rejoined the group around Horgan.

'Don't tell me you're going soft,' Tracy said.

'What do you mean soft?'

'You were almost gentle with Brogan.'

'He's not a bad lad.' She downed her drink 'Time to suck up to the boss.'

Horgan had his back to the bar and he was launched into some story where he was either the hero or the anti-hero. It didn't much matter. Fiona needed to be away and was afraid that the narrative would never end. She pushed into the group. 'Thanks for the drink, boss.'

Horgan stopped in mid-sentence and looked at her. 'You're not away, are you? The party's only getting started.'

'It's been a long day. Tracy and I have been up since the crack of dawn. I can't keep my eyes open and Tracy has to drive me home.'

'That's a pity.' He turned back to his admirers and continued his story from where he left off.

Fiona rejoined Tracy. 'Let's get to hell out of here. They turned to leave.

'Fucking dyke.' It was whispered but loud enough for them to here.

Tracy was about to turn but Fiona held his arm and continued towards the door.

'Whoever said that shouldn't get away with it,' Tracy said.

'I know. But you trying to sort it out wouldn't help. Remember, most of them think it.'

'You shouldn't have to put up with that in this day and age.'

'They're not living in this day and age.' Fiona gave a middle finger behind her back as she left the bar.

CHAPTER SIXTY-NINE

Fiona leaned against the window of the car. She was exhausted. She'd hardly eaten in seventeen hours and her emotional tank was running on empty. She'd called Aisling from the car and gave her the news.

Aisling told her she sounded exhausted and to hurry home.

'She won,' she said, more to herself than Tracy.

'Who the hell cares. I just want to go home and take a long shower. I thought it wasn't about winning and losing. We don't do the justice bit. The DPP will look at all the evidence and draw their own conclusions. Maybe Phil and Nevens will tell another story. Right now I don't give a damn for the Connors, Nevens, Horgan and the whole damn lot of them.'

'Welcome to real life. It's better not to care too much. It's a survival strategy in our business. You show them that you care and you give them the power. Take my advice and never give away your power cheaply.'

They were silent as they approached Fiona's cottage.

'Are you meeting Cliona tonight?'

'We're having a meal later.'

'Don't forget to thank her for her help.'

'She likes you.'

'Nice girl, bad judge of character.'

'She can't believe that you're gay.'

'She'll have to meet Aisling.'

Tracy pulled up in front of Fiona's cottage.

She opened the passenger door.

'Don't forget the prawns. I don't suppose I've told you that I enjoy working with you.'

'No, you didn't.'

'Well I do'

'I'm glad you're my partner, Tracy.' She slapped him on the shoulder. 'You're one of the good guys and there aren't many of you out there.' She opened the car door. 'Tell Cliona I'm asking for her.'

Tracy popped the boot. 'Don't forget the prawns.'

Fiona smiled and went to the rear of the car. As soon as she closed the boot, Tracy drove away. She watched the car until it disappeared. 'Don't go soft on that boy, Fiona,' she said.

WHEN SHE WALKED in the door, the smell of roast something already filled the room.

Aisling came from the kitchen and put a glass of Prosecco into her left hand while taking the bag of prawns from her right. 'I'll put these in the fridge. You look all in.'

'It's been a tough week. What are we having?'

'Lamb, roast potatoes and veg. And a nice bottle of Chianti.' She did her bad impression of Hannibal Lecter before she disappeared into the kitchen.

'That was an awful attempt at a Anthony Hopkins' impression.' Fiona sat on the couch and sipped her drink. She realised why she loved Aisling. She was the perfect antidote to melancholy. Tomorrow it would all start again. They would spend the next month building their case against Maggie and Phil Connors and Luke Nevens. Then she was going to an island and forgetting about the shitty job she had to do and the arseholes she had to do it with. Her eyes were beginning to close when she saw something on the coffee table. She recognised it instantly. It was an age-stained page from the *Galway Advertiser*. The headline read GALWAYMAN'S DISAPPEARANCE BAFFLES GARDA SÍOCHÁNA. 'This newspaper on the coffee table,' Fiona said. 'Where did it come from?'

Aisling came from the kitchen. 'Dinner in fifteen minutes. Someone pushed it under the door. What does it mean?'

'I haven't an idea. Perhaps someone thinks I take on cases on a personal basis. They don't know much about the Garda Síochána.' She folded up the paper and held out her glass. 'Top me up and when that's finished, top me up again.'

DID YOU ENJOY THIS BOOK?

If so and you'd like To try my Wilson series go to my website, https://www.derekfee.com and sign up to receive the first two books in the series FREE.

Thank you for your support.

AFTERWORD

Author's Plea

I hope that you enjoyed this book. As an indie author, I very much depend on your feedback to see where my writing is going. I would be very grateful if you would take the time to pen a short review. This will not only help me but will also indicate to others your feelings, positive or negative, on the work. Writing is a lonely profession, and this is especially true for indie authors who don't have the backup of traditional publishers.

Please check out my other books , and if you have time visit my web site (derekfee.com) and sign up to receive additional materials, competitions for signed books and announcements of new book launches.

You can contact me at derekfee.com

ABOUT THE AUTHOR

Derek Fee is a former oil company executive and EU Ambassador. He is the author of seven non-fiction books and sixteen novels. Derek can be contacted at https://www.derekfee.com.

Printed in Great Britain
by Amazon